MURDER HAS A HEART

A KELLY ARMELLO COZY MYSTERY BOOK 6

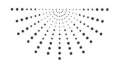

DONNA DOYLE

D1607628

PUREREAD.COM

CONTENTS

MISCHIEF IN THE SHELVES

"**L**ook at this!"

Kelly Kennedy, the library director, looked up from the circulation desk to the balcony where Chloe Grissom, the children's librarian, stood.

"Isn't that Raggedy Ann?" Kelly asked.

"Why is Raggedy Ann wearing a bikini?" Carmela Dixon, the library technician, holding an armful of books to be shelved, asked.

It took a couple of minutes before Kelly, from her vantage point, realized that Carmela was accurate. Raggedy Ann, the familiar children's literary character, was indeed wearing a bikini over her pinafore. The bikini top, black and clearly sized for an adult human and not a children's rag doll, was positioned at a disadvantage to the doll, but it was, at first glance, somewhat amusing.

Carmela made the mistake of emitting a snort of laughter. Kelly, wiser in the ways of the sensitive and volatile children's librarian who had not yet recovered from the Christmas break-up with her fiancé, did not.

"Who would have done that?" she asked. "Carmela and I were here on Saturday morning, but we didn't notice anyone—well, I guess we wouldn't have noticed," she realized. Chloe worked part time and her scheduled days were Tuesday, Wednesday and Thursday, but she often stopped in on Saturdays when the library was quiet to work on decorating or planning programs. The Children's Corner was her realm, and Kelly and Carmela knew that she was territorial about the room.

"The Shaw kids were up there with their mother on Friday afternoon after school," Carmela said. "But they weren't up there an unusual amount of time. And I asked Mia to turn the lights off on her way down."

"The Kessners came in after that . . . they turned on the lights, but they didn't make a mess. They never do. Everyone who was in the children's corner was a regular," Kelly recalled. "I went up to turn out the lights but I didn't look around the room to check the displays."

"I had heart-shaped confetti spread all around a display of books about love," Chloe continued. "And someone brushed all the confetti to the floor. It's a mess, all over the place!"

"This is the Sloans' weekend to clean," Kelly said reassuringly. "They'll sweep it up."

"Someone moved all the books about love and put in monster books!" Chloe was not to be mollified. "I had a perfect Valentine's Day arrangement in the story circle and now it's a mess."

"Just clean it up as best you can," Kelly said kindly. "No one will be in on Sunday, and the Sloans will clean it all up. Someone was just playing a prank."

"Someone unhappy in love," Carmela offered. "Not everyone is looking forward to Valentine's Day. Not everyone is a newlywed," she said with a side glance at Kelly.

"Troy has to go to a police officer conference in Harrisburg. He won't be back until next weekend. We were supposed to go to the First Responders'

Valentine's Dance but he doesn't think he'll be able to leave until Sunday."

"You can go to the dance anyway," Carmela said. "I'm going."

"Why don't you invite that nice Mr. Porter," Chloe, her ill-humor forgotten for the moment, asked teasingly. "I bet he'd love to go with you."

"I can go on my own," Carmela said. "I'm not tied down and I'm not going to a dance with a man who's been collecting Social Security since before I paid off my house!"

There seemed to be no correlation between the two events and Kelly's eyes met Chloe's in a shared glance of puzzlement.

"Well, he seems like such a gentleman," Chloe said.

"Maybe he put the bikini top on Raggedy Ann," Carmela said grumpily as she stomped off to put books away.

"Oh, he would never do something like that," Chloe protested. "He's a gentleman."

Her comment received another derisive snort from Carmela, unseen but heard from the stacks.

"Gentleman! That's just a polite way of saying he's an old man!"

"No, it's not," Chloe insisted. "A gentleman can be any age. There just aren't very many of them around."

As Chloe and Carmela continued to voice their disparate opinions on what constituted a gentleman, Kelly's gaze remained focused on the circulation database, but her thoughts were far away. Troy Kennedy, her husband of only a few weeks, was scheduled to attend the police officer conference in the Pennsylvania state capital. He was still not fully recovered from the gunshot wounds that had nearly cost him his life last year, but physical therapy, a rugged constitution, and marriage had done as much healing, his doctor said, as the surgeries and hospital care. The town of Settler Springs had taken Troy Kennedy into their hearts after his bravery in exposing the criminal deeds of the previous police chief, Roger Stark, who was now in prison awaiting trial, along with his wife and his brother-in-law, the previous mayor. When former police officer Leo Page had been voted in as mayor, his first act had been to talk to the members of the town council about naming Troy as the new police chief, a decision with which the council had been unanimously in favor. Troy hadn't been certain at first; he hadn't been in the town all that long compared to other potential candidates, and he still wasn't one hundred percent back to speed . . . but Leo had insisted, and Kelly had been enthusiastic when Troy broached the idea.

They'd both been disappointed when the week of the police officer conference was scheduled to end on Valentine's Day. Troy knew he could drive easily back in time for the dance, but Kelly didn't want him to hurry. Still mindful of the injuries from which he was recovering, Kelly told him that his health was much more important than a dance.

"I'll make it up to you on Sunday," he promised. "Chocolates, roses, a fire in the fireplace and any romantic old movie you want to watch."

She smiled as she thought of that promise. Troy didn't like the romantic old movies that she enjoyed; to make that offer was either a husband's guilt or genuine regret that he wouldn't be with her on Valentine's Day.

"What—I suppose someone thinks this is funny!"

Carmela's indignant voice emerged from the stacks moments before she herself came out, holding a pair of wine glasses in her hands.

"In the 100s," she said grimly.

Kelly frowned in bewilderment. "Not the classification I'd have chosen for a romantic tête à tête," she said. "Those books don't even go out very often."

"Five of them did," Carmela said. "But they weren't checked out in the system. Someone just took them."

"And brought them back?'

Chloe had gone back into the Children's Corner to repair the damage done to her display, leaving Kelly and Carmela alone in the main library.

Carmela shrugged "They were in the drop this morning from outside," she said. "Someone must have dropped them off after we closed last night because that drop was empty before we left."

Kelly didn't doubt that Carmela had taken care of all the books that had been returned during the day. Carmela was religious in her adherence to her tasks and emptying the drop before closing the library was one of them.

"I don't know when the glasses were there," Carmela said, sounding aggrieved. "There's barely any circulation from this area and I haven't shelved books here for days. Maybe weeks. Of course, we were closed for Christmas week," she said, "and once we opened, the kids were busy with their second semester reports. I haven't paid much attention. The wine glasses were behind the books . . . I only noticed them because I was shelving the ones from the drop."

"They might have been left there from that wine and cheese party we hosted after Caroline and Keith opened their winery," Kelly remembered. "I'll bet that's where the glasses came from."

"That's probably it," Carmela said, relieved that the mystery was solved. "People were all over the place. We did pretty well with that fundraiser."

"I think Caroline and Keith are going to be good for Settler Springs," Kelly agreed. "They've already proven that they're library supporters with that fundraiser." She and Carmela went on to discuss the new couple that had opened their winery in Settler Springs and gave every indication that they would be active in the community.

"I wonder if they'd like to do one for St. Patrick's Day," Carmela said.

Kelly laughed. "I think we'd better let a little time go by before we ask them to do a second fundraiser," she said. "They'll need to concentrate on getting their business started. They have that Dinner for Two night for Valentine's Day."

"If the snow doesn't ruin everything."

"What snow?'

"There's a big storm coming this way," Carmela told her. "Didn't you see the forecast? It's supposed to be a blizzard out west and by the time it gets here, we could end up with a foot of snow."

"I hope not," Kelly said. "Troy will be coming back from Harrisburg on the weekend."

"Oh, don't worry about it," Carmela said, immediately changing her tone when she saw that Kelly was concerned. "You know how the weather forecasters are, they're always wrong. I wish I had their job. Get paid lots of money and it doesn't matter if I say it's going to rain and then it's sunny out."

2

AWAY FROM HOME

Troy checked into the hotel, brought his luggage up to his room, turned on the television and began to unpack. He'd be at the conference all week and while he wouldn't be wearing his police uniform, he didn't want to look too casual in his attire. It had been a cold winter so far, and the temperatures had given no indication that they would rise any time soon.

Troy put on The Weather Channel so he could listen to the forecast while he hung up his clothes.

"Winter Storm Sergei is beginning to make its appearance in the West and by the end of the week, it will have travelled all the way to the East coast, leaving blizzard conditions, dangerously icy roads, and the heaviest snows we've seen this year.

Travelers are warned now to expect flight delays as Sergei moves across the nation, and if you're not traveling, you'll want to make sure you're prepared in case the power goes out—"

Troy paused in the midst of hanging up a shirt as he ran an inventory in his head of his winter preparations at the house where he lived, but which he still thought of as Kelly's house. There was ice melt and rock salt in the garage. The trunk of Kelly's car had a shovel, cat litter, road flares, a blanket—

He smiled. Kelly knew how to take care of herself. She'd been doing it before they got married in December and, as she was fond of telling him, she had been shoveling snow from the sidewalks and clearing snow off the windshield before she became Mrs. Troy Kennedy. His smile deepened. All that was true. But what was new was the comfort of curling up together beneath the quilt that Kelly's great-grandmother had made, warm and cozy together, while the snow fell, soft and slumberous, outside.

It would be a week of waking up without Kelly's bright red hair splashing like warm flames on the pillow next to him, and a week of—

He was going to miss her. He hadn't known that love could be like this, and he had certainly never, not in his wildest imagination, expected that married love was anything like what he felt for Kelly. It was like being a willing hostage to a woman whose smile made coffee and toast in the morning seem like a buffet. Why didn't anyone tell a bachelor that a red-headed woman in a plaid flannel nightgown that looked like something out of *Little House on the Prairie* could, on a bitterly cold winter's night, evoke the same effect as the cover on the *Sports Illustrated* swimsuit edition?

He'd gone into marriage with no illusions and plenty of experience with women. But somehow, none of that mattered with Kelly Armello because, in her arms, he was the novice, the student who was learning about love from a woman who had never shared herself with any other man but him. He wasn't sure how that happened; all he knew was that what he felt for Kelly was an emotion that defied description. It was something hewn out of passion, certainly; he didn't deny that Kelly set his heart racing, whether they were seated across from each other in their booth at The Café after a morning run, or whether she was entering the living room with a bowl of popcorn, or whether she was wearing what she called her "cleaning comfies"—the baggy sweatshirt and sweatpants that she donned when she was mopping the floor. It didn't matter. Which meant, he supposed, that passion was more than a stunning redhead with a gorgeous figure and long, lovely legs. Of course, he loved her, but love wasn't adequate to encompass all that he felt. Love was a word on greeting cards; it failed to convey the soothing presence of a woman who had sat beside his hospital bed while he was unconscious from wounds that could have killed him. Love wasn't a big enough word to describe the woman who had come into his life as a pest, determined that he would help her prove the innocence of a boy accused of murder and then, over the span of months, somehow left a trace of magic upon every aspect of his existence. Kelly was greater than love, she was the reason that valentines were sent and the—

Valentine's Day! It still rankled that he'd had to go on a conference that would separate them on Valentine's Day. How that would have amused Sean Claypool, his army buddy; cynical Troy Kennedy, upset because he was going to miss his first Valentine's Day as a married man.

It was still difficult to think about Sean, his friend, who had been killed as part of Chief Stark's vendetta against Troy in an effort to warn the determined police officer to abandon his quest for proof of Stark's involvement in the drug trade. It was because of Sean that Troy had moved to Settler Springs. The town had been where Sean had grown up until he was ten, when his parents divorced and he moved to Texas with his father. Sean had spoken with genuine nostalgia for the town and when Troy got out of the army, he had no particular destination in mind, so Settler Springs, Pennsylvania, seemed as good a place as any. Growing up in a peripatetic military family, Troy didn't know much about putting down roots.

Kelly had changed that. Settler Springs had changed that. Now he knew the people of the town; he knew that the Krymanskis were much more than the criminal clan that Chief Stark and Mayor Truvert had labeled them. He knew that Mia Shaw was trying so hard to overcome her past as a drug user so that she could prove that she was ready to be a mother to her kids again. He knew how much Jimmy Patton, the paramedic, cared about the people he brought to the hospital.

Troy felt bad that because of this conference, Kelly would have to miss the First Responders Bowling League Valentine's Dance. Jimmy had put it all together; he'd gotten Caroline and Keith Rancotti to give him a good price on the wine for the event and because it was as much a fundraiser as a holiday dance, they had been glad to do so. Doug Iolus, who was as close to a Renaissance man as Settler Springs had, was volunteering his services as the deejay for the night. Local restaurants—The Café, Sloppy Joe's, The Pizzaria across the river—had joined forces to have the dance catered, not with burgers and pizza but with steak and shrimp prepared by a relative who was glad to help out the town's first responders.

It was kind of funny, Troy reflected, that the First Responders Bowling League, which had begun as a somewhat covert group for people who were all engaged in trying to prove that Roger Stark's activities were criminal and that he was using his position to profit from the drug trade rather than trying to prevent it, had become such a success that there was now a Valentine's dance planned as a fundraiser. It was indicative of the way that Settler Springs had become his home instead of just the next stop on the map of his life. Kelly's close ties to the town had forged a sense of belonging that he had never experienced before. But then, so much of his life now was transformed because of Kelly.

It was close to suppertime. But before he went out to get something to eat, he reached for his cell phone.

Her voice, when she answered, was eager and anticipative, as if she'd been waiting for him to call. "Hi, you got there okay."

"No problems getting here," he said, stretching his legs out on the ottoman in front of the chair.

"Carmela says there's a winter storm coming this week," she said, sounding worried.

"Sergei."

"What?"

"Sergei. Winter Storm Sergei. You're the library lady, you're supposed to know all these things," he teased.

"I know," she said, as if she thought he was serious. "I didn't know about it until Carmela said something today at work. If it's too bad, don't try to come home next weekend, okay? You don't have to be on the roads if they're bad."

"I'm here for a week," he said calmly. "There's no sense in worrying about a storm that's just now revving up in the West. Don't worry. I might not be home in time for the dance, but I'll be home for Valentine's Day night."

"I've got a whole list of movies lined up to watch," she said.

"Um. All black and white, I suppose."

"Of course. They're more romantic."

"Uh-huh," he replied, not disguising his dubious response. "You'll owe me for this."

He could imagine her as she sat on the couch, her warm smile curving at her lips as they talked. He'd read somewhere that a person's conversational tone was influenced by whether or not they were smiling as they spoke on the telephone. Kelly's smile came right through the cell phone towers. "I'll do my best to pay. . . ."

"Run some of your payback ideas past me and I'll let you know if they'll pass muster for a night of black-and-white movies."

"Candlelight?"

"Good idea in case the power goes out."

"If the power goes out, we won't be watching movies."

"In that case, I'll be in charge of the entertainment, so you don't have to worry."

She laughed. It was warm and cozy and intimate. "A bottle of wine. We don't need electricity for that. Oh, speaking of wine, you'll never guess what Carmela found in the stacks today when she was shelving books."

"A bottle of wine left over from the fundraiser the Rancottis did at the library last month?"

"No, but you're close. At least I think you are. There were two wine glasses in the back of the shelf where Carmela was shelving the books on marital infidelity. We're thinking someone left them there after the fundraiser."

"It's strange that she just found them. I thought Carmela was relentless at keeping the shelves in order."

"Those books don't go out much," Kelly explained. "It was just peculiar, especially after someone put a bikini top on Raggedy Ann."

Troy burst into a laugh. "A bikini top on Raggedy Ann? What kind of library are you running, woman? I'd say somebody needs to check this out."

"Chloe was so upset. She had a display in the story corner with books on love. Someone put them to the side and filled the display with books on monsters. And they spilled all her heart-shaped confetti all over the story rug."

'Wow, you've got an anti-Valentine's Day parent lurking in the library."

"It's the Sloans' weekend to clean; they'll take care of the carpet and Chloe can put the display up again and everything will be back to normal."

3

NEWCOMERS TO SETTLER SPRINGS

Caroline Rancotti stopped in the library on Tuesday morning to see Kelly. The short, vivacious woman, her sandy blonde hair disheveled from the cold February wind, entered Kelly's office in her customary dynamo style.

"Kelly, what if the snowstorm is so bad that it cancels the dance?" she asked, without a greeting, as she sat down in the chair opposite Kelly's desk.

"I keep forgetting to check the forecast. Carmela said it's going to be a bad storm."

"A horrible storm, a blizzard," Caroline wailed, her hands punctuating the air as she reinforced her dismay. "I had The Weather Channel on and they're saying there are going to be hundreds of cancelled flights all the way to Philadelphia! They're getting ready to shut down the highways if it's as bad as they expect, and governors in some of the states are telling people to prepare to stay home and not go out on the roads. This could really wreck the dance!"

It was typical of Caroline that a snowstorm of such power would immediately translate into how it would affect a dance that she and Keith were supplying the wines for, but Kelly understood the woman's concern. They were just in the process of getting their business going in town, and the First Responders Valentine's Day Dance was an opportunity to showcase their wines for some of the town's most influential citizens.

"Maybe it won't be as bad as they're saying," Kelly said soothingly. "That happens sometimes, you know. We all rush to the store to stock up on bread and milk and toilet paper and then the storm fizzles out."

Caroline shook her head emphatically. "Not this one," she said with certainty. "It's going to hit. They all agree."

"I hope not," Kelly said. "Troy will be coming home from a conference in Harrisburg Saturday evening."

"Saturday evening? Will he get home in time to come to the dance?"

"No," Kelly said. "I don't want him to rush home, and the last day of the conference is when he'll be in groups with other small-town police chiefs. He wants to hear what they're doing on how to tackle some of the problems that small towns share."

"But you'll be at the dance, won't you?'

"Not without Troy."

"Oh, but—" then Caroline subsided. "No," she said at last. "I guess I wouldn't want to go to a dance if Keith couldn't come too."

"But Carmela will be there," Kelly said. "She could even have an escort for the night. There's a wonderful gentleman who comes into the library every afternoon to read the newspapers, and we think he has a thing for Carmela. He's asked her to join him for some of the activities at the senior center."

"Oh, that's sweet. Is she bringing him?'

Kelly was free to speak because Carmela was on her lunch break and was not in the library. "No, she thinks he's too old. She's going solo."

"But why not take him if he's interested in her?"

"She says he's too old," Kelly repeated.

"Is he?"

"Well . . . he's not young. But he's very fit and Chloe calls him a gentleman. I think he's a dear," Kelly confided. "I know he's older than Carmela, but he's very sweet."

"Did he just suddenly show an interest in her?"

"He's new to Settler Springs," Kelly said. "He just moved to town after Christmas. His sister used to live here, and when she died, he came to settle the estate. He likes it here, he said. He says it's very peaceful after life in the city."

"He wouldn't have thought it was so peaceful if he'd been here when all that dirty business with the Starks was going on," Caroline said. She and her husband had moved to Settler Springs the previous fall, and even though they'd been busy renovating an old church to transform it into a winery, they had each followed the events with trepidation, wondering if they'd chosen the wrong location for their business. Fortunately, the misdeeds of Chief Stark had been exposed and the town was returning to normal, thanks to the dedication of people like Jimmy Patton, the chief of the ambulance service, and Leo Page, now the mayor, and, Kelly was proud to add, her husband Troy's dedication to his work in law enforcement.

"He missed that, although I guess he's from the city so maybe it wouldn't have seemed unusual to him."

"You'll let me know if plans for the dance change?" Caroline asked, standing up to leave.

"Jimmy will be the one who'll decide," Kelly said. "He'll make sure you know."

"I hope the storm goes south," Caroline said. "Oh, that reminds me. Thanks for referring your cleaning service to me. I trust them completely. They clean everything; Keith always checks for cobwebs, but he never finds any, so he's decided that we'll stick with them. But what I was going to say about the storm going south . . . Jessie Sloan is pregnant!"

It was no use trying to conjoin the destination of the storm with Jessie Sloan's reproductive state. "She is? That's wonderful news! I know they've been hoping to have a child but they've been so disappointed so far."

"Yes, Greg told me when he came by to pick up his check. But he's concerned about her being able to carry the pregnancy to term, so he told her she needed to go and stay with her mother in Tennessee and he'd take care of the cleaning. He doesn't want her to be around the cleaning chemicals or doing any heavy lifting. He did it all himself this week, so it doesn't look as though there's going to be any drop in the work. How do you pay him?'

"How do I—?"

"I mean, we're open over the weekend and I know he's cleaning offices then."

"Oh, I see. We have a mailbox for him in the back room and I just leave his check there. He picks it up when he comes to clean."

"You pay him before he cleans?" Caroline seemed surprised by this unorthodox business arrangement.

Kelly laughed. "The Sloans have been cleaning the library for the last three years and they always do a good job, so it's never been a problem. If I want them to give a particular area a special cleaning, I leave a note. They have a key and they come in on their own schedule, every other week, so it doesn't disrupt anything going on in the library."

"Oh, of course. I gave them a key when they started so they could come in on their own hours, but I never thought of having a place to put notes or a check. That's the perfect solution."

"Is Jessie going to be in Tennessee for the whole pregnancy?"

"Greg says that's what she wants. She's from Tennessee, did you know that? She wants to be with her mother, he said, and she's comfortable with the doctors down there."

It seemed unusual to Kelly that a woman would choose to be away from her home for a pregnancy, but as she thought of the slender, soft-spoken woman with that lilting drawl in her voice, and thought of the miscarriages that she'd suffered, she realized that she couldn't blame Jessie for wanting to make sure that this baby would be all right. "What about Greg? He's going to miss her, and she'll miss him. I'm not here when they clean, but I know from the times I've seen them together that he's devoted to her."

"Oh, he's going to visit regularly, he told me that his cleaning schedule might change sometimes so that he can go down to see her and be part of the pregnancy."

"She must be very close to her mother," Kelly said thoughtfully, "to want to be there with her instead of up here with her husband."

"Oh, wait until you and Troy start a family," Caroline promised. "You'll want your mother with you, too. My mom and I used to fight all the time when I was a teenager, but after I got married, and then when I was pregnant with Emily, I went to my mom for everything. She and Keith were in the delivery room with me for Em and for Nora. It's something that you'll understand when it's your turn."

Kelly smiled, but after Caroline left, she thought about what she'd said. Her parents lived in Florida for much of the year and came up north for the Thanksgiving and Christmas holiday season before returning to their Orlando condo. She would definitely want her mother to be involved in her pregnancy once she and Troy were at that point in their marriage, but she knew that she would never want to be apart from Troy for as long as Jessie was going to be away from Greg. It was commendable that he was so tolerant of that time frame. Of course, she reminded herself, the Sloans had endured much disappointment as they waited for a successful pregnancy to bring them the baby they desperately wanted. Who was she to think that she had any idea of what kind of heartbreak they had experienced?

Marriage was such uncharted territory, Kelly realized. She and Troy, each in their own way, were finding out together that love turned a couple into pioneers, blazing a new trail in a world that was filled with such possibilities. But, as the Sloans had found out, it was not always an easy journey. She would have to send Jessie a card soon, to congratulate her on the happy news.

4

LUCAS IN LOVE

Lucas Krymanski typically showed up at the library one day a week to see if Kelly needed him to do anything. What had originally begun as community service hours punishment after he and friends had gotten caught "egging" the mayor's house had turned into a regular habit for the fifteen-year old, partially out of gratitude for Kelly's role in preventing him from being falsely charged for murder. But Lucas had found a home in the library community and he and the often-gruff Carmela had bonded after Mrs. Stark, the former library board president, had banned Lucas from the library. That of course was before she'd been arrested for the part she had played in her husband's involvement in the drug trafficking scandal that had led to murder and political corruption. Now that she was no longer in residence at the library, Lucas entered freely.

It was a quiet Wednesday afternoon. The preschool story hour Valentine's Day party had been the highlight of the day and Chloe had been pleased with the enthusiasm of her group. She had left for the day and Carmela was gone as well; Wednesday night was choir practice at her church. Kelly was at the desk when Lucas came into the library. He gave a quick glance to see who was present: there was Mr. Porter, sitting in the reading section with the day's newspapers; several patrons were browsing the new book displays; a student was at the computer station doing research.

Lucas appeared satisfied with the population. "Hi, Miz Armello," he greeted her. Lucas knew she was married but he seemed to be oblivious to the fact that her last name had changed, and Kelly didn't bother correcting him. "Do you need me to move any tables or anything?"

"Hi, Lucas, good to see you. There are a couple of boxes of books that need to be brought upstairs to the storage shelves. We're not doing any programming; just the regular story hours."

"Okay," Lucas said. He knew where everything was located and quickly took care of the tasks. But instead of waving goodbye and getting on with his evening, Lucas loitered at the circulation desk. Kelly waited on two of the patrons while Lucas continued to stand at the circulation desk.

"Miz Armello," he said, "can I ask you something?"

"This is a library, Lucas," Kelly smiled. "Go for it."

He frowned in concentration, glanced around the library again to make sure that no one was in earshot, then, lowering his voice, asked, "Do you love Officer Kennedy?'

Kelly's eyes opened wide. "That's why we're married," she said, intrigued by his question.

"Yeah," he nodded. "I figured that. But how did you know you loved him? I mean, you weren't dating or anything when you were solving all those murders, and then he was in the hospital. He wasn't even conscious for a while. So what was it that told you, y'know, that you loved him?" Lucas spoke in a rush of words as if he were releasing them from captivity.

Kelly tried to interpret the thought process that was driving Lucas' mysterious curiosity about love. "Is this about me loving Troy," she asked delicately, "or about something a little bit more personal?"

Lucas averted her gaze. "I dunno," he said finally. "You know Madison Boarts?"

"Maddie? I know her, she's part of the Gamers Club, along with you and the others. She's a pretty girl," Kelly said tentatively, unsure of where Lucas' conversation was heading.

"She's tall."

"Is she? I suppose she is," Kelly, who was tall herself, hadn't really noticed Maddie's height.

"She's taller than me," Lucas said gloomily.

"Not much. Besides, girls stop growing before boys do. She's probably reached her full height, you probably haven't."

Lucas looked at Kelly as if she were speaking a foreign language. "No?"

"Probably not." Lucas had that look that she recognized from other teenage boys she saw in the library, the appearance of limbs that were gangly and stretching, waiting for the full accommodation of bone and muscle to achieve their destined length.

"Girls are done by now?"

"I was tall when I was a teenager, but I'm wearing the same size shoe that I wore when I was a sophomore in high school. At the eighth-grade dance, I was taller than all of the boys. And then, when it came time for the prom . . . I wasn't."

"You're shorter than Officer Kennedy."

"We're not running a contest on who is taller," she said in amusement. "But yes, he is taller than me. He weighs more than me. He has bigger muscles than me. He's a man, what do you want?"

Lucas joined in her laughter as if a great weight had fallen from his shoulders. "Yeah, I guess so . . ."

"She's a pretty good gamer," Kelly said slyly, wondering how Lucas felt about regularly being bested in the monthly tournaments by the girl who was taller than he was in height and superior to him in playing video games.

"Yeah," he said proudly, "she's better than any of us. She's a girl, but she beats us all."

Good for you, Lucas, Kelly thought silently, for not minding that a girl can beat you.

"She's pretty good," Kelly allowed.

"You know she wants to go to college to learn how to create video games? I didn't know you could go to college to do that."

"Some colleges have that program in their curriculum. I suppose there's a lot of other talents involved."

"She's on the honor roll in school."

"You know a lot about her," Kelly said, deliberately keeping her tone nonchalant. Maddie was one of the group of teenagers who came to the library for the monthly video game tournaments; most of those attending were boys, but there was a handful of girls, including Maddie. Kelly hadn't noticed anyone paying any particular attention to anyone in what she would have considered a romantic manner, but there wasn't much romance in gaming, at least not that she'd detected. But then, the previous year had been so fraught with events that she'd failed to notice that Lucas, a skinny fourteen-year old when she had first met him, was now going on sixteen, taller—even if not as tall yet as Maddie—and more grounded. His sister's drug addiction the previous year had put him in the unlikely role of her protector. Now, with Carrie out of rehab, working and going to college, he was free to return to his carefree ways. But it seemed as though Cupid had found him.

Lucas shrugged. "I guess," he said noncommittally.

Had Maddie noticed Lucas as anyone but another one of the gaming group? Perhaps not. Maddie was a pretty girl, a smart girl, but not a frivolous one. She had long, thick blonde hair that she wore in a messy bun; she didn't seem to care that her glasses failed to show off the startling blue of her eyes; her denim and tee-shirt attire was clearly worn for her own comfort. She was, nonetheless, quietly self-confident, a girl who knew who she was and seemed to have a clear sense of personal direction.

"Do you have any classes together?"

Lucas shook his head. "Just a study hall," he said. "She's always doing homework."

Lucas, his quest for answers about love apparently answered to satisfaction, took his leave then, promising to stop by the following week in case the library needed him. Kelly smiled as she watched him walk out of the library and take his bike from the rack. Then, like the Lucas she was more familiar with, she watched as he rode the bicycle down the library steps, even though the sign posted on the bike rack forbade riders to do so. The snow that had fallen that morning was mostly cleared away, but Lucas didn't let the remnant hinder him from his daring.

As she watched, she saw Greg Sloan coming up the steps, pausing to call after Lucas, no doubt scolding him.

"Hi, Greg," she greeted.

"Crazy kids," Greg said, shaking his head. "He could get hurt and then what would happen? The library could have a lawsuit on its hands."

"More likely that Lucas would be grounded for the rest of his teenaged years, after he recovered," Kelly said philosophically. "His mother knows her son well. She'd fly into him for riding the bike down the stairs."

"Maybe," Greg said, sounding doubtful. Maybe he believed, like much of Settler Springs, that a Krymanski was naturally culpable. It was a preconception Troy Kennedy had done much combat, but there were town residents of long standing who were hard to convince. Greg had been born and raised in Settler Springs. He'd gone to community college nearby but somewhere on the way, he'd gotten distracted by love, met Jessie on an out-of-state trip south, married her and started his own cleaning business.

Greg generally picked up the Sloans' paycheck on the weekends that they cleaned and in truth, the staff rarely saw the Sloans. Kelly supposed he was there to tell her that he'd be working a different schedule, now that Jessie was with her mother and he'd be visiting her when he could, but she didn't want to admit that Caroline had divulged the happy news about the baby.

Her guess was correct. "I'll be changing my schedule," he told her. "I'm—we're . . ."

He seemed uncomfortable in bringing up the subject. Impulsively, Kelly said, "I understand you have some exciting news."

Greg looked startled.

"About the—Caroline Rancotti told me," she admitted. "I was so happy to hear that Jessie is expecting. I'll have to send her a card congratulating her."

"Not yet!" Greg said hastily. "She's—it's early yet, and—"

"Oh, of course." Naturally Jessie was hesitant and would be until the first trimester was over. "Of course. You'll tell her that she's in my prayers?"

"I will, but don't—she doesn't want people to know yet. I didn't know Mrs. Rancotti would tell anyone."

"She just wanted to let me know that your schedule would be different because you'll be going down to see Jessie. That's fine."

"I'll be gone this weekend," he said. "I'm going to try to get away before the snow comes."

Kelly didn't want to admit it, but the more she heard about the forecast, the more anxious she became at the thought of Troy away in Harrisburg. "Travel safely," she said. "You might want to leave as soon as you can to beat it."

Greg nodded. "I've got my office clients to do tonight and the school tomorrow afternoon, and then I'll take off tomorrow night."

"Thanks for stopping to let me know, and congratulations."

His face twisted and Kelly realized that for Jessie and Greg, the prospect of pregnancy was forever tinged with worry that this one, too, would end in miscarriage. But Greg, who was quiet by nature, the opposite of his chatty, engaging wife, just nodded.

Kelly wondered if she should put Jessie on the prayer list at church but then decided not to. It was plain that Greg didn't want the word to get out until he and Jessie were sure that this baby would make it past the first three months of pregnancy and they deserved their privacy.

She wondered if she'd be as reticent, when the time came and she and Troy were expecting. She thought she'd likely want to shout it from the rooftops from the moment she knew, but maybe not. Maybe there was sense in waiting. At any rate, it wasn't anything she had to consider now. She and Troy weren't going to start a family yet, not with him just starting his new position as the police chief and so soon recovered from his injuries.

To everything, there is a season, she thought. A season for Lucas to fall in love, and the Sloans to hope for a successful pregnancy, and for her and Troy to enjoy being newlyweds.

5

THE APPROACHING STORM

By Thursday, the weather reports were so grim that Jimmy Patton decided to cancel the dance. The storm was moving steadily, burying the Midwest in the amounts of snow that meant treacherous travel, closed schools, and gloom among florists and restauranteurs who realized that the lucrative Valentine's Day holiday was going to be a weekend of shoveling out, not dining out.

"There's no sense in waiting," Jimmy said, stopping in at the library to update Kelly. "It'll be here by Friday, if not sooner, and by Saturday we'll be plowing out from under just like they are in Illinois and Nebraska."

"I think that's the right thing to do, Jimmy. We might close early today. Carmela and I both have things we can do from home. I just hope Troy has the sense to wait in Harrisburg until the turnpike is safe."

Jimmy's broad features relaxed into a smile. "Kelly, if there's one thing Troy has in abundance, it's sense. He's not going to risk his life to travel when it's not safe."

Kelly tried to look as if she were confident that Jimmy was right. "I hope so," she said again. "He's just now starting to feel a little better and I don't want him . . . I don't want anything to happen to him."

"He's a smart guy," Jimmy told her. "He'll stay put. I better be moving along, I've got a few more people to disappoint with the news. It's too bad about the Rancottis; they were looking forward to showing off their wines. Well, it can't be helped. See you around, Kelly."

"'Bye, Jimmy."

"Don't worry, Kelly," Carmela, who had been at the desk during the conversation, assured her. "Jimmy's right. Troy's smart enough to stay put."

"It's not that he isn't smart enough, he just thinks he can handle anything that comes along. I told him how, a few years ago, the snow was so bad that the turnpike closed, and cars were stranded for hours. The National Guard had to come out and help. He thought it was funny; he said that'll probably happen sometime on his Guard weekend!"

"He was probably just trying to keep you from worrying."

"He wasn't successful!"

Carmela's comforting tone altered when a dapper, elderly gentleman with a trim white mustache approached the desk and removed his hat. "Good morning, ladies. I wonder if the latest issue of *Sommelier* has come in yet?"

"If it had," Carmela said churlishly, "it would be out on the rack with the other magazines."

Mr. Porter was used to Carmela's brusque nature. "Of course," he said urbanely. "I only thought that, if it had come in but not been processed, that I might prevail upon you to let me see it."

"Of course we would, Mr. Porter," Kelly told him warmly. "We'd be happy to. But it's not in yet. You'll be careful, won't you, with this snow coming? You'll stay inside and you won't shovel?"

"Oh, I like the snow. I lived for twenty years in Las Vegas before coming here, so I'm quite looking forward to a good snowfall. My neighbor is a fine young man and he plows my driveway. Isn't that kind of him?"

"You shouldn't be driving if it's going to snow as much as they say it will," Carmela admonished him. "What happens if you get stuck somewhere and a tow truck has to come and pull you out? Or worse, what if you get in an accident and the ambulance has to take you to the emergency room?'

"My dear Miss Dixon, thank you for your solicitude. I intend to sit by the fire, reading my book and enjoying a hot toddy while I watch the snow fall outside my window. I'm quite looking forward to it. You will, also, I hope, be careful?"

"I'm used to winter," she retorted.

"We're closed on Sunday and Monday; Monday is Presidents Day, it's a holiday. If it snows a lot on Friday, like they're saying, we'll also be closed on Saturday," Kelly answered him, once again interjecting a note of cordiality to offset Carmela's grumpiness.

"Very good, then. Is there anything I can get for you ladies in the meantime?" Mr. Porter included both women in his question but his eyes lingered on Carmela, who ignored him.

"Thank you, Mr Porter, that's very sweet, but I went to the grocery store last night and stocked up, and I'm sure Carmela is prepared as well."

"Then I wish you both a Happy Valentine's Day, and a pleasant winter weekend," he said as he donned his hat and gloves and turned to go.

"Oh, Mr. Porter—" Kelly called.

He turned.

"Thank you again for the flowers," she said. "They're beautiful. We don't get roses for Valentine's day from our other patrons."

"It is the very least I can do for all the kindness you have shown me." He raised his hat in farewell, his gaze once again idling on Carmela who either pretended not to notice or genuinely did not see.

"Chloe is right," Kelly said after he was gone. "He really is a gentleman."

Carmela made a noncommittal sound of disdain as she continued to process books sent by the district's interlibrary loan circulation.

"I wonder what he did in Las Vegas," Kelly pondered.

"Probably worked at a casino," was Carmela's guess. "He's smooth enough."

"I still don't understand why you've taken against him," Kelly protested. "He's always so polite. Courtly, I would say. And he certainly does think highly of you. Even though those flowers were sent to both of us, I'd be willing to bet a breakfast at The Café that he had you in mind when he ordered them."

"I'd be a fool to think that and he's a fool, at his age, to be doing outlandish things like that. Sending us roses, for heaven's sake," Carmela said with a frown as she picked up the stack of books. "He's probably living on Social Security, at his age, and now he'll have to eat Ramen Noodles for a month to make up for what he spent on those roses." She glared at Kelly. "I'm going to call everyone and tell them that if they want the books they ordered, they'd better pick them up before we close. And I'm telling them that we're closing early. If that storm speeds up and the snow comes overnight, we might not be open tomorrow."

"Good thinking," Kelly agreed. "It's not supposed to get here until overnight Friday, but if people are going to be inside for a long weekend, they'll want their books with them. Tell them that we're closing at two. You and I can make up the time working from home."

She was looking forward to a mystery novel by a newly published Scottish author, although how much reading she'd get done while worrying about Troy was a mystery of its own. The novel was set in the wintertime in Victorian Scotland, and under usual circumstances, Kelly would be eager to begin reading. Troy would take a look at the cover and tease her, asking whether she didn't think she'd had enough mysteries in her life. 'But these are cozies,' she'd tell him, as she always did. 'It's entirely different.'

He'd shake his head and go out into the kitchen. Soon, she'd hear the sound of popcorn popping, and he'd return with a bowl that he'd place on the sofa between them to share. He'd find a sports event to watch on television, she'd glance up now and again, if it was a hockey game, then return to her book. The comfort of those evenings assailed her now.

"I just want him home safely," she whispered to herself. "Dear God, please make him be sensible and stay there until the storm has passed."

When she went home after work, she sat in front of the television to listen to the weather report. The storm, the forecaster said in tones that were better suited to announce the imminent approach of an advancing army than to give a weather report, was picking up speed and was expected to arrive sooner. "If you're going to go out for milk and toilet paper," the forecaster, a sober, suited man with an unsmiling demeanor warned, "you'd better get it soon. This storm could very well hit overnight, making travel treacherous for the morning commute. But the road crews plan to be out salting overnight and they'll do their best to keep travel safe."

Kelly's thoughts were a jumble: *Troy at the conference that was to end midday on Saturday; Greg Sloan, leaving tomorrow to be with his pregnant wife; Mr. Porter, prepared to enjoy winter weather that would seem exotic after years in sunny Las Vegas; Jimmy, wise to have cancelled the Valentine's Day dance; Chloe, who would be mournful that she hadn't gotten flowers this Valentine's Day; Carmela, for some reason disgruntled that she had gotten roses; Lucas, struggling with the chaos of his first love; Troy . . .*

"Please, Lord," she prayed as she rose from the couch and went to look out the window at the dark skies, "please bring him home safe to me."

She reached for her cell phone to call Troy, but there was no answer. She knew, because he had told her, that a group of officers usually went to dinner together. She didn't feel like eating supper; instead, she made a bowl of popcorn and turned on The

Weather Channel, to watch as the forecasters told the saga of Winter Storm Sergei's march to the east.

6

BEATING THE STORM

"As we used to say in the Army, it's better to ask forgiveness than ask for permission."

The officer who was in charge of the conference smiled sympathetically. "Forgiveness from your wife or from the conference? Go home, Kennedy. But be careful. If the storm comes fast, it could be causing trouble on the roads you'll be traveling. Don't be a hero."

"I'm not trying to be a hero," Troy said. "I just want to get home and wish my wife Happy Valentine's Day."

The officer nodded. "Go and pack and take off," he said. "I'll send your certificate to you."

"I packed this morning," Troy grinned, "and everything is loaded and ready to go."

The officer put out his hand. "You bring a lot of experience to law enforcement," he said. "I think your community will be pleased to have you in command."

Troy was in his Suburban fifteen minutes later and on his way home. The weather forecasts were ominous, but he didn't want Kelly to know that he was leaving early, or she'd worry that he'd be caught in the storm. Better not to answer the phone call, he thought, as he stopped to fill up the Suburban's gas tank before getting on the turnpike. If he called, she'd be able to tell that he was in the SUV and not in his room. He didn't want Kelly to worry about him. Afghanistan had snow too, he'd reminded her, and he'd driven on far worse roads than any in Pennsylvania. He had emergency supplies in the back if he needed them. He still had some of the brownies Kelly had baked for him to take to the conference, so he would have something homemade to enjoy. The container was on the passenger seat now. He got hot coffee and two hot dogs from the convenience store, and when he got back into the Suburban, he texted Kelly.

Getting supper now. I'll talk to you tomorrow. I'll take care of the shoveling after I get home, and I know Lucas will take care of it if I don't beat him to it. I love you.

It wasn't a lie, he reasoned as he took off a glove so that he could eat the hot dog while he drove. Kelly didn't need to know that supper wasn't at a table in the hotel dining room, or even room service by himself. A hot dog in the front seat was still supper.

He'd watched the news and listened to the weather forecast. Winter Storm Sergei had picked up momentum and was expected to hit earlier than previously forecast, striking into the early hours on Friday rather than Saturday. If it continued to retain its strength, it was likely that school in Settler Springs would be cancelled on Friday. But that wouldn't bother Lucas Krymanski, who would be out with his shovel, bright and early, to earn money. He took care of the library's sidewalks because his mother told him to, but the library parking lot was too big an area for a kid with a shovel. Troy knew that Lucas would show up at the door of their home to shovel for Kelly and that he wouldn't take money for that either. Not because Tia Krymanski told him not to, but because Lucas refused when Kelly tried to pay him. Which was one of the reasons why Troy tried to get to the snow right away, rather than have

Lucas do it for free. But if the storm got an early start, he might not be home in time to do the first round of shoveling. Kelly reminded Troy that she had done her own shoveling before she married him and she could do it again.

And she probably could, but Troy didn't want her to. He wanted to get home safely, and then he wanted to make sure that she was safe too. The library closed when the school closed, so he wasn't worried about that. The borough truck would be out plowing and salting, and traffic in town was likely to be light, Troy knew. But still, now that he was chief of police, he didn't want to be away when his community would need him. Kyle wouldn't be able to make it into the station; Troy didn't expect him to try. The risk of falling as he transferred from his vehicle to his electric scooter was too great. The new guy, Hayden Croft, was good, but he was new. Troy had talked to Leo about the possibility of adding a part-time officer to the budget and Leo was going to see what the council could do. When Troy first started with the Settler Springs Police Department, it was a four-man outfit, so upping the roster back to that number wasn't an outrageous request.

Have a good supper. Stay there, don't take a chance on the roads with this storm. We'll have our own Valentine's Day when you get home. I love you.

Troy smiled as he read Kelly's response to his text. He intended to be home before Valentine's Day, surprising Kelly. And right now, there was no sign of the storm to come. He was confident that he could get home to Settler Springs before it got too bad. Things might get a little dicey closer to home if the storm hit early, but the Suburban could handle snow and Troy wasn't a novice at winter driving.

Troy stopped along the way to refill his coffee so that he'd stay awake. After he'd driven for an hour, light snow began falling. Troy turned on his windshield wipers. There wasn't much traffic on the turnpike, which wasn't surprising, considering that it was already night and travelers would be staying close to home. The snow began to fall a little more heavily.

Weather forecasters, Troy thought resignedly. Always wrong. Not only was the storm coming earlier, but it wasn't even waiting for overnight.

He pulled off the exit ramp to get a refill on his coffee. As he did so, he noticed a vehicle stranded on the side of the highway. A man was standing beside his van.

"Need any help?" Troy rolled down his window.

"A flat," the man said. "I'm trying to beat the storm, but this is going to slow me down."

"You have a spare?"

"Yeah, I already got it out of the trunk."

"Hang on, I'll give you a hand," Troy said. He pulled over and parked behind the stranded car.

"That's—thanks," the man said.

"No problem. You have a jack?"

"I—no, it's broken."

"I have one, hang on. I'll get it."

Troy got his equipment from the Suburban and, taking the spare that the man offered, set to work. The ground was snow covered already, and he had to be careful to avoid sliding on the wet surface. The man wasn't much help as he stomped his feet to keep them warm and wrapped his arms around himself to ward off the cold. It didn't look as if he was prepared for winter; Troy's assessing gaze noticed that the jacket didn't look like it was meant for cold weather, and the man was wearing sneakers, not boots or anything with a tread.

"There, that should do it," Troy said as he stood up and brushed snow off his jeans. "You traveling far?"

"I'm going to find a motel and spend the night," the man said.

"Good idea. Are you set up for travel in this kind of weather? Do you have a blanket in case you get stuck somewhere? Something to drink?"

"No, but I'll be fine," the man assured him.

"Hang on," Troy said. "I'll give you mine."

"Oh, you don't have to do that," the man protested. He seemed eager to get going and Troy couldn't blame him, with the snow coming faster and harder. Still, it was better to take the time to be prepared for the roads and the cold in case he was stranded.

"It's all right, I have extras." Troy, always prepared, didn't just have emergency supplies in the SUV, he had back-up emergency supplies. He handed the box to the man who seemed surprised at Troy's offer. "Just in case you need it," Troy said.

"I—can I give you something?"

Troy didn't expect anything and doubted that the traveler had enough money for the turnpike tolls, judging from the way he was dressed.

"There's no need," he said. On an impulse, he went back to the Suburban and brought Kelly's container of brownies with him. "Here, have these. My wife made them for me and I've had plenty."

"Your wife?"

"My wife, Kelly. She loves to bake."

The man thrust the container back. "I can't take these, not if they came from your wife," he said.

"It's okay, she won't mind. I've had plenty."

The man shook his head. "She made them for you. That's something special. Thanks for your help, I'm going to be on my way now."

"Be careful," Troy said, puzzled. The man was already in his car when Troy realized that they hadn't exchanged names.

It didn't matter, he thought as the car pulled back onto the highway. He hoped the guy got to where he was going without any further trouble. Troy smiled as he got back into the Suburban and put the brownies back on the front seat. Wait until he told Kelly that someone had passed up an offer to sample her double-fudge walnut brownies because the guy didn't think something from a man's wife should be shared with anyone.

7

HOME SAFE

Kelly awoke when she heard Arlo growl. The German shepherd, who slept at the foot of the bed, had been moping since Troy left for the conference, but in an instant, he was off the bed and racing down the stairs.

"Arlo? It's just snow," Kelly called after the dog. It wasn't like him to act this way when he needed to go out. Sighing, she put on her bathrobe and slippers and followed Arlo downstairs. "Wait until I put on my coat. I'll take you out."

She donned her thick winter coat and leashed Arlo, then opened the door. "Oh, my!"

The houses across the street all had white roofs. Every car on the street was encased in white, its color concealed by the snow. The street was white with no tire tracks marring its pristine surface. The snow fell in swift waves of white, an uninterrupted flow from the sky blowing as the cold wind stirred the thick flakes as they descended. The snow soundproofed the night. It was, in its way, beautiful, Kelly thought as she stared up at the sky.

"Arlo!" she said to summon the dog back. "Come on now, it's cold out here. Do your business and let's go back inside."

But Arlo, his ears perked up as if he were listening to something, ignored her. He prowled back and forth in the yard, his purpose forgotten.

"Arlo!" Kelly whispered fiercely. "Come on, it's cold."

She saw Arlo stand as if at attention, as the glow of headlights from a vehicle illuminated the snow. Then the lights drew closer and Kelly stared as the vehicle pulled into the driveway.

"Troy!" she shouted and, heedless of the fact that it was snowing and she was wearing slippers, she hurried down the porch steps, through the yard, to greet her husband as he was getting out of the Suburban.

"What are you doing home?" she demanded. "You were supposed to stay in Harrisburg until the storm passed. You have snow all over your hair," she said, reaching up to brush the snowflakes away.

"So do you," Troy said. "Now, let's get inside before we both freeze out here."

Arm in arm, with Arlo in front as if he were leading the procession, they went up the steps and into the house.

"You told me you'd stay there until the storm was gone," Kelly accused him as she helped him take off his snow-covered, fleece-lined jacket.

"No, *you* said I was going to stay there until the storm was gone," he corrected her, laughing. "I decided I'd beat the storm."

"But the conference doesn't end until Saturday!"

"I'd bet my paycheck that I'm not the only guy who decided to skip out early and head home rather than deal with traffic tie-ups and bad roads."

"It started early," she said. "I'll make coffee. You must be freezing. And hungry. I'll make you something to eat."

"Kelly," he laughed, taking her coat off and pulling her into his arms. "If there's one thing I don't want, it's more coffee. I've been drinking it the whole way here. It took me longer than I thought it would because the storm got ahead of the forecast."

"Hungry? Are you hungry?"

He was hungry; the hot dogs had worn off. But he wasn't so hungry that he wanted Kelly to be making him a meal in the middle of the night.

"I'm just hungry for you," he said, holding her close. Her red hair was wet from the snow that had fallen and her slippers were soaked. In her red flannel nightgown and her white terrycloth bathrobe, her curls mussed, she was the most beautiful woman he'd ever seen, and he wished he had the words to tell her that.

She fit into his arms as if they had been engineered to embrace her. "You should have waited until the storm was over," she said, her voice muffled against his chest. "But I'm so glad you're home. Arlo heard you! Before you were here, he heard you. I was asleep and suddenly he growled. The next thing I knew, he was going down the stairs. I thought he wanted out, I didn't know it was you. Are you sure you don't want coffee?"

He only convinced her that he didn't want anything to eat or drink by lifting her off the ground as he went upstairs. "I just want to fall asleep with you beside me," he said, putting her down when they reached the landing.

"Me, too," she said with a smile as they went into the bedroom, arm in arm, with Arlo leading the way.

Kelly was awake after Troy got out of the shower and got into bed, Arlo giving a disgruntled sound as he was forced to move over to accommodate Troy's length.

"I've only been gone a few days and he's already taking over my side of the bed," Troy joked as he pulled the covers back over himself, tugging them loose from beneath Arlo, who emitted another sigh of canine exasperation.

Kelly snuggled into his arms. "I was worried," she said. "But now that you're back home and safe, everything is okay. Were the roads bad?"

"It wasn't bad when I was leaving. The storm hadn't hit Harrisburg yet. By the time I got to this end of the state, it was a little treacherous."

"I don't think you can use the words 'a little treacherous' together," she objected, marveling to herself at the comfort that she derived from Troy's physical presence. It was more than desire or the appeal of his rugged frame, she realized. It was the alchemy of knowing him as well as she did, and the anticipation of continuing to know him, while the intimacy of their bond grew deeper. "Did you have any trouble?"

"A little sliding here and there. Nothing to worry about. I'm hoping people stay off the roads tomorrow. I'll go in to the station to keep an eye on things. I don't want Kyle to chance it. Haydon will be in. I'm going to talk to Leo about hiring a fourth officer so we have enough to rotate shifts."

It was soothing to hear Troy talk of the everyday topics of his work, but for Kelly, the thought of him on the long turnpike route from Harrisburg to home was still in her thoughts. "Were the road crews out?"

"They were, but the snow is falling pretty fast. Too fast for them to keep up with it."

"You didn't run into any trouble?"

"Me, no. But there were a couple of other people who needed some help. One couple had slid off the road and needed help getting back on. And there was a guy who had a flat tire, an hour or so after I got out of Harrisburg. I've lost track of the time. It took longer to get home than it did to get there because of the snow. He sure wasn't dressed for the weather."

"You helped him?"

"He was on the side of the road with a flat. He already had his spare out, but he didn't have a jack. I stopped, changed the tire. Poor guy; he had on sneakers and didn't have a winter coat. Gloves, either." Troy shook his head. "Why he'd be on the turnpike in this kind of weather, without being dressed for winter, I don't know."

"Where was he going?"

"I don't know. He said he was going to find a motel and stay for the night. I hope he did. He shouldn't travel too far on a spare."

"What if he can't find a motel?"

"I left him my spare box of emergency supplies. I tried to give him some of your brownies, but when he learned that my wife had baked them, he said no. That's the first time anyone has ever said no to your brownies."

"He didn't want to eat them because I baked them? Did you know him?"

"No, he was a stranger. I mean that he didn't think it was right to eat something that my wife had baked for me."

"Maybe he's going to visit a girlfriend for Valentine's Day," Kelly suggested.

"Maybe, although a girlfriend who wouldn't forgive a guy for eating brownies baked by another woman has some pretty tough standards," Troy noted, kissing the top of Kelly's head where the riot of uncombed curls burst out upon the pale green pillowcase.

"Oh, I don't know," Kelly said as if she were giving the matter serious thought. "If the way to a man's heart is through his stomach, then baking for him is pretty serious."

"I ate most of them anyway," Troy said. "His loss."

"Maybe his girlfriend will bake him some," Kelly said confidently as she kissed the rough edge of Troy's chin. "You need a shave."

"Tomorrow," he answered. "Tonight, at least for what's left of it, I just want to hold you in my arms and go to sleep."

Kelly was happy with this agenda. Troy fell asleep quickly and the silence of the bedroom was punctuated by his even, measured breathing, Arlo's sleep sighs, and from outside, the noiseless sound of the falling snow. This was perfection, she thought as her mind, finally able to relax now that Troy was home safe and in her arms, reflected upon the pleasure that this moment afforded her. It was as if they were in their own private snow globe, snug and warm within, secure in their love for one another. With Arlo at the foot of the bed, guarding their affection.

The whimsy made her smile. Troy was sound asleep, Arlo was spread out on the foot of the bed, mostly on her side now that he had to contend with Troy's extra height for sleeping room. Neither was thinking of anything. Only she was awake to ponder the mystery of love and the intricate ways in which the small things became so important. Troy was home. He was safe. Everything was all right.

8

THE WINTER WORLD

The next morning, she stole silently out of the bed, dressed quickly and quietly in the bathroom so that she wouldn't wake Troy, and whispered for Arlo so that she could let him out.

The sun hadn't risen yet, and even when it did, Kelly knew that the day's illumination would mostly come from the frigid brilliance of the snow as it lay everywhere, casting its eerie pure light upon the street. It was beautiful, in its own way. She would take Arlo for a walk later in the afternoon. By then, some of the sidewalks would have been cleared of snow and the streets would have been plowed, although with the snow still falling, she wasn't sure that walking would be any easier. But she had sturdy boots and warm pants and a thick sweater, and with gloves, a scarf and a hat, she'd be outfitted for the season. She gave a fleeting thought to the people that Troy had helped. Lucky for them, she thought as Arlo came back up the porch steps, not eager to linger out in the cold, that Troy had come by. What a night for a flat tire, and to be out in this kind of weather without proper winter attire. It made her doubly appreciative of all that she had, and as she went back inside, savoring the warmth of the house after the outdoor chill, her thoughts were on the day ahead.

She'd make a big pot of vegetable soup, she decided, for supper. And she'd bake bread to go with it. She didn't bake bread that often, but she knew that Troy loved eating fresh bread with butter smeared and melting on it. First, though, was breakfast. As she diced potatoes for home fries, and cracked eggs into the frying pan, she smiled, remembering what Troy had said about the man who hadn't eaten her brownies because something made by a man's wife was for the husband to enjoy. It was a strange concept, but as the bacon sizzled in the pan, joining the aromas of the other foods, she knew that cooking for Troy was something that brought her a private pleasure. If she were honest, she'd have to admit that the thought of another woman preparing breakfast for him would bother her.

"I bet Angela never made you breakfast," she mused aloud to herself as she put toast in the toaster.

"No, she didn't."

Kelly twirled around. "I didn't hear you. I was going to come wake you up."

Troy grinned. "With the smell of bacon in the air, you think I needed you to wake me up?"

He buried his head in her neck. "That should be in the wedding vows," he murmured. "Love, honor, cherish, and make breakfast."

"It only counts if it's done freely," she said. "Now you can make the coffee while I finish up here."

After the hotel breakfasts, it was good to be back at home, in the kitchen nook where he and Kelly had their meals in front of the side porch window where they could watch the birds taking gluttonous advantage of the bird feeder that Kelly filled faithfully when it was empty. He was looking forward to the view when the seasons changed and there would be leaves on the trees that were now shorn of their foliage.

"You've got a lot of talents, Kelly," Troy said as he eagerly tucked into the full plate Kelly had placed before him. "But the way you make bacon might just be tops. It's a hard call though. And to answer your question, no, Angela didn't make breakfast. What made you think of her?"

Kelly's cheeks held a faint blush of pink. "Oh, no reason," she said.

"There's no reason to think of her," he said firmly. "This—he waved his arm around the kitchen, encompassing the food, the view from the window, and Kelly, "this is more than I knew would ever be possible. I didn't know it was even there to want, and I sure didn't know how much I wanted it until we were married. Besides," he added, "Jarod Zabo was much more present in your life than Angela was in mine."

"Okay, okay, we can nix the exes," she said, laughing.

"Good. Did you ever cook breakfast for Jarod?"

"You know I didn't," she exclaimed.

"Just making sure," Troy grinned. He sat back in his chair. "We're lucky, aren't we?"

"Did you just realize that?"

"No, I realize it every day. It's just that it's a revelation every day." Troy drained the last sip of his coffee. "On that note, I'll get out and shovel before I go to the station."

"You know that I can shovel snow," she reminded him.

"I know you can. But I owe you for that breakfast. It'll probably snow again, so if Lucas comes by, see if he'll take money for doing it."

"I'll try. I'll probably stop by the library later. He might have already done the library, he usually gets an early start when there's a snow day and he's off school."

"He might have to give it a couple of shovelings," Troy predicted. "It's still coming down."

"Will you come home for lunch?"

Troy's grin was answer enough. "I'm hoping for a nice, slow day," he said. "With a nice, long lunch."

After Troy finished shoveling the sidewalks and the driveway, he left for the police station. Kelly put the breakfast dishes in the dishwasher and started on the bread and soup she was planning for supper. Around mid-morning, after adding thick socks and boots to her attire and bundling up in her ski jacket, she prepared to go to the library. Arlo, who had taken to perching himself in front of the door, gave her a mournful look.

"I guess it won't hurt if you come with me," she said. "The library's closed anyway, and you're a good dog."

Arlo knew what good dog meant and although he was disappointed that this time it wasn't accompanied by a treat, he was mollified by the leash that signaled a walk. Outside, the world was still a winter wonderland. Arlo found the landscape to his liking; the snow, which was an impediment when he was let out to answer the calls of nature, was now an adventure, and he eagerly trotted ahead of Kelly so that he could sample the soft, white paths that had replaced the sidewalk pavement. Wind blew snow down off the branches onto his nose and he looked around himself in surprise, turning his head to see if Kelly was responsible.

She laughed at him. "It's snow, Arlo," she said. "You've seen it before." Not, she had to admit, like this. This was the kind of snowstorm that didn't show up very often. It looked as if they already had about ten inches of snow and it hadn't stopped falling. This was going to be a disappointing Valentine's Day for the restaurants and florists. Although it was too bad that the Bowling League had cancelled the Valentine's

Day Dance, she thought Jimmy had been wise to do so in advance. This year's celebrating would be an in-the-home event. But that wasn't so bad, she thought. Having Troy home, when she'd expected that he'd still be in Harrisburg, made the holiday all the more worth anticipating. Maybe she'd bake chocolate cake. . . . Troy would like that. She wasn't sure what she'd make for their meal; she hadn't shopped for anything special because she hadn't expected him to be home. This wasn't a day for grocery shopping.

The sidewalk in front of the library was snow-covered, but the path was narrow and already white again. Higher heaps of snow were on the road and in the yard. Lucas had been by to shovel. There were no footprints anywhere, not on the sidewalk or the steps or the porch. She doubted if anyone had come by, even if they wanted to drop off books that were due. On a day like this, people would stay inside until the snow stopped and then they'd venture out to clean off their cars and shovel their sidewalks. There was a protocol to snow in Settler Springs.

No one else was out. She felt as though she and Arlo were the only living creatures in existence. It was not an unpleasant sensation, this deep sense of peace that winter evoked. Everything was veiled in white: the branches on the trees in front of the library looked as if they were dressed for a wedding; the hedges that bordered the library were topped with white snow; the remnants of last year's flowers were solitary in their white covering. Snow gave the world the time it needed to pause, she thought, for a quiet celebration. There was no rushing in winter. There was only this serene peace and the feeling that the world was taking a break from its busy schedule.

"Okay, Arlo, we're going to go inside but we won't be long. I just need to empty the book drop, make sure the heat is okay, and then we'll be back on our way. So you behave yourself, okay? Maybe we'll stop at the station on our way back and see Troy."

She patted the German shepherd, who seemed friskier than usual; Kelly supposed that the snow was having an effect on him. She unlocked the side door to the library; Lucas had shoveled here, fortunately; the wall of snow to the side of the door revealed how much snow had blocked the entrance before his efforts. That was the only evidence that anybody had been near the library. The neighbors were all inside, snug in their homes, sheltered from the cold. And once she finished here and got back to her house, she and Arlo would be able to enjoy the comfort of inside as well.

9

FINDING THE BODY

Inside, the library was still. Kelly turned on the lights. "Arlo, sit," she said when the big dog began to get restless, pulling at his leash. "Why are you misbehaving?" He was always so well behaved, even for her, although it was Troy that he acknowledged as his master. "This just isn't like you."

She hooked his leash over the back of the chair before going to the drop to pick up the books that had been dropped off the night before. Arlo began to bark as she moved away from him.

"Arlo!" she said in exasperation. "I don't know what's the matter with you! You're—"

She abruptly halted. As she approached the fiction shelves, she spotted shod feet, heels up, sticking out past the edge of the shelving unit. For a brief, frozen instant, Kelly stood where she was, unable to move. Arlo had stopped barking. She turned around to look at him; the dog was staring at her with an alert expression in his eyes.

"Arlo. . . ."

She took her cell phone out of her coat pocket. Then, before she began to press the numbers to call Troy, she ended the call. She couldn't just call him without telling him what she had found. Maybe it was someone, maybe—

"There wasn't anyone in here last night when we left," she said aloud. "There shouldn't be anyone in here now." She pressed the numbers on the cell phone and this time, she didn't hang up first.

Troy answered on the first ring. "Hi, Kelly, I'm already getting hungry thinking about that—"

"Troy, there's a body in the library," Kelly spoke in a rush, needing to get the words out before she stopped to think about what she was saying.

"Is anyone in the library?"

"I don't think so. Arlo is with me."

"Okay. I'll be there in minutes. Leave the library and go outside," he said. His voice was calm but she knew him well enough to realize that he was going into police officer mode, dispending information and instructions with dispassionate authority.

"Okay, I just—"

"Go out of the library now. Start walking and leave the library, and cross the street. I'm on my way."

"C'mon, Arlo," she said after he had hung up. "Let's go . . ."

The dog whimpered as if he perceived her emotions. He seemed reluctant to leave, however, turning his head to look in the direction where she had seen the body. But he was obedient to her commands and left the library with her.

She was shivering as she waited for Troy across the street, but it wasn't from the cold. When the police car pulled up to the sidewalk, Troy emerged, leaving the car running, but she walked to him as if she were unable to maneuver her limbs.

"He—he's in there, in the f-fiction unit, I was going back to the b-book drop, Arlo was bark—barking, but I didn't know why, he was even acting strangely when we were outside, before—before we went in, I thought he was excited because of the s-snow—"

Troy took her in his arms for a brief, fierce hug. "I left the squad car running," he said. "Go ahead and get inside and get warm."

"I don't want you going in there alone!" she said, suddenly protective, her fear gone.

"I won't be alone," he said, taking the leash from her hand. "I've got Arlo."

"But—"

"Kelly, get in the car and stay inside. Let me check it out. Maybe . . . maybe it's not what it seems."

She brightened. Maybe it was a prank. Maybe someone had dressed up a dummy and left it in the library as a joke, like they'd put a bikini on Raggedy Ann. But who could get into the library to play a prank like this? No one would do that, the board members wouldn't, the Sloans wouldn't, the staff wouldn't. . . .

"In the car, get warm, okay? I'll come out as soon as I can."

She obeyed his instructions and got into the car. He hadn't put the police lights on, for which she was thankful. The neighbors might notice the car, but they weren't likely to think there was anything ominous in the presence of the car. The neighbors knew that Kelly was married to the police chief, they'd probably assume that he had stopped by to pick her up or take care of some minor errand, they wouldn't think he'd come to the library because she'd found a dead person—a man, the shoes were a man's shoes, she hadn't seen much of the body but she'd seen the feet. She should have known that Arlo had a reason for behaving as he had, all his instincts were on alert for threats, it was his nature, and he'd known. She'd scolded him, but he'd been trying to warn her; he was such a good dog, she'd have to remember that the next time—"

She buried her face in her hands. Next time? What was she thinking? There was a dead body in the library, this wasn't something that betokened a next time.

Tapping on the window jolted her out of her grim reverie. She looked up. Lucas was standing outside the police car door, shovel in hand, looking concerned.

She wasn't sure how to lower the window so she opened the door.

"Miz Armello, you okay?" he asked. "I did the sidewalk this morning, I was coming around to give it a second shoveling. You okay?"

"I—I'm fine, Lucas," she said, teeth chattering.

"You don't look fine," he said with a boy's blunt assessment. "You look like something's wrong."

"I—"

"Is Officer Troy here?"

"He's—he's in the library."

"Why's he in there and you're out here?" Lucas wanted to know.

"I—"

"Miz Armello," Lucas said when she didn't finish her sentence. "What's going on? Something's the matter. You want me to go in and check on Officer Troy?"

"No! No, don't go in there, Lucas! Just—just—"

"You want me to shovel it again, or wait until later?'

"Wait—no, don't wait, don't shovel—"

"Miz Armello, what's the matter?"

She didn't want to cry in front of Lucas. She was the grown-up. She had to remain composed. "There's—I think someone's been hurt," she said, trying to prevent her teeth from chattering."

"In the library? How? It's closed."

"I know. I don't know. I called Troy to check."

"I can go in and help."

"No, no, you stay out here, you—you go ahead and shovel the other sidewalks. Mrs. Nardiscio, she's older, she can't do her walk. She'll pay you to do it."

"I'll do it," he said. "But I'm not leaving you alone. Do you know how to open the back doors of this car?"

"No, I—I don't know how to do that. Troy knows. I'm sorry, Lucas."

"Maybe I could sit in the driver's seat," he suggested, sounding eager.

"I don't think that would be a good idea," she said, smiling despite the situation. "You don't have a driver's license and if the car mysteriously started to move—"

"Look, Miz Armello, it's the other cop! The new guy," he announced as Hayden Croft pulled up behind them.

"I'd better—"

She started to get out of the car, but Hayden waved her away. "Just stay there, Mrs. Kennedy," he said. "Lucas, you'd better go on home."

"I can't leave Miz Armello," Lucas said.

But Hayden was no longer listening. He was walking purposefully up the ramp leading to the side door of the library entrance.

"Miz Armello, he has his gun drawn!" Lucas said, alarmed. He looked at Kelly, his expression serious. "You'd better tell me what's wrong," he said, sounding much older than the teenage boy who had first become a library volunteer because he'd been caught egging the mayor's house as a Halloween prank.

She decided to open the door and get out of the car. It wasn't fair to Lucas for him to be outside in the cold while she was inside.

"I went in to take care of the books that were left in the drop overnight," she said matter-of-factly, forcing herself to relay what had happened as if she were simply giving an account of why she had been there. "Sometimes before a storm, people like to drop off their books in case they won't be able to return them before they're due." She gripped the open police car door, leaning on it for support.

He nodded. "So what happened?"

"I had Arlo with me, you know Arlo, and he was acting strangely, then he started barking." She began to shiver again and wrapped her arms around herself to try to stop the movement. "I—I went back to the drop, you know where it is—"

"I know."

"And I saw, sticking out of the shelving, back where the fiction starts, I saw—two feet, with shoes. Men's shoes."

"Who was it?"

"I don't know—I called Troy and he's in there now."

"You think there's a dead body in the library?"

"I think—it's someone."

"How'd he get there?" Lucas wanted to know. "You and Miz Dixon closed up last night like usual, didn't you?"

She nodded. "Everything was just the way it always is, except we put the sign on the door that in case of snow, we'd be closed during the day. The forecast said it would be coming early so we wanted to be prepared."

"Yeah, I figured we wouldn't be having school today so I left my history book at school."

Kelly was diverted by this unexplained comment. "What does your history book have to do with school being closed for weather?"

"We were going to have a review for a test next week in history class," Lucas said, smiling as if he were divulging a brilliant idea. "I figured we wouldn't have school today, so I left my book in my locker. Mr. Patrice will have to postpone the test because we wouldn't have time to study for it."

"Wouldn't you have had time to study if you brought it home and studied over the weekend?"

Lucas' expression revealed that Kelly's suggestion wasn't her brightest contribution to the conversation.

"Why would I do that?"

"Why indeed," she said, smiling. Somehow, Lucas Krymanski had a gift for bringing the subject back to a more prosaic, less harmful, center of gravity.

THE INVESTIGATION BEGINS

W hen the state police car appeared, lights flashing, Kelly knew with a sinking heart that whatever was going on in the library now had passed the stage where she could hope that it was all just a misunderstanding with a simple explanation. Following right behind was the vehicle marked Coroner. Then another vehicle. She watched them arrive and park in front of the library, moving into the building with the kind of purpose that belonged in mystery novels but not in the Settler Springs Public Library.

"Wow, Miz Armello, that's the state police!"

"I know," Kelly said. She recognized Trooper Susan Callahan, the state police officer who had risen in the ranks after Trooper Meigle had been arrested as an accomplice of Police Chief Stark. Trooper Callahan was a taciturn, no-nonsense officer with a military background, like Troy had. And who was, incidentally, a highly competitive bowler, having joined the First Responders League while Troy was still in the hospital recovering from the wounds he had suffered when Stark and Meigle had tried to kill him.

Trooper Callahan wasn't thinking about bowling scores now. She nodded to Kelly, but said nothing as she passed them on her way into the library.

"Miz Armello. . . ."

"I don't think the person in the library . . . he's dead. . . ."

"If the police are here, he's more than dead, Miz Armello. He musta been killed."

Kelly winced at the words, even though she knew that Lucas was only voicing the truth she wanted to avoid. Not in the library. The library to Kelly was almost a sacred place, second only to her church, a place where the community's needs were met in a way that only the library could provide. Murder— her mind flashed back to the other murders that had taken place: the girl in Daffodil Alley; Lyola Knesibt on Groundhog Day in Punxsutawney; John Parmenter at the lake where Leo Page had his camp; Sean Claypool, Troy's army friend . . . murder had been the ugly backdrop against which she and Troy had met and gotten to know each other and, against the expectations of either of them, fallen in love. But those terrible crimes had happened elsewhere, in other places. This was in her domain, the library, the place where children came to hear stories and teens came to take part in gaming competitions and genealogists came to explore their family histories and students did research and Mr. Porter came to read the newspaper and Mia Shaw picked out Dr. Seuss books for Mason and Lucia and—

She watched as she saw Troy emerge from the library and cross the street. When he approached her, his face was grave.

"Kelly . . . I'm sorry . . . we need you to see if you recognize the man. I'm sorry."

She nodded numbly. She had known this was inevitable. They had to identify the body and they assumed that she would recognize the man. It was logical. A dead body found in the library was surely a patron.

"Miz Armello," Lucas said, noticing her ashen features and clumsily trying to help.

"It's okay, Lucas . . . you should go on with your shoveling. A lot of people are going to need your help. There's so much snow . . ."

"But—"

"Lucas, you can come by the house later," Troy said. "We'll know more then."

Lucas looked to Kelly. "You gonna be okay, Miz Armello?"

She nodded, not trusting herself to speak. "Troy is right. You can come over later."

"Okay," he said, his hands on his shovel. "I'll see you later, then. You look out for her?" he asked Troy.

"I will." At another time, Troy might have found the request amusing. But he knew that Lucas was feeling protective toward Kelly. "I'll look out for her." Lucas was no stranger to the evil that men could do, Troy reflected. There was a patina of unexpected wisdom over the youthful countenance; in time, it would become a part of him, and probably make him a better man, when he was of an age to be a man. He had been wrongfully accused of murder, kidnapped by men who were in the pay of the corrupt Chief of

Police Roger Stark, and he'd seen his sister nearly die of an overdose. Now, once again, murder was making an appearance in his life, and in a place that the boy associated with safety.

Troy wanted to shield Lucas and Kelly as well from the ugliness of murder, but that was beyond his power. "Is The Café open?"

"Sure, Mom's there. She walked to work. She said people will want to come in for meals, like always, and talk about the snow."

"Why don't you go there?" Troy suggested.

"No, she'll set me to work shoveling the sidewalk," Lucas declared.

"It's probably shoveled by now. Go on, Lucas, I'd rather you were with your mom."

"I'll go there when I've finished shoveling," Lucas bargained. "This whole street needs shoveling. I'm saving for a car."

"You're not driving age yet," Troy said, trying to keep a light tone. He could feel Kelly shaking beside him and he sensed that it was more than cold affecting her.

"I will be!"

"Okay, go ahead and shovel, and then go to The Café."

"Mom . . . she'll want to know what happened here."

For of course, Troy knew, the neighbors peering out their windows would already have phoned their neighbors with the news that the police were at the library.

Troy shook his head. "There's a murder investigation taking place," he said.

It was enough. Lucas' eyes widened. "It seems like there's a lot of those in this town. I thought they were done with murder after the Starks were arrested."

"I have to get Kelly inside," Troy said.

Lucas nodded, but he didn't move from his spot as he watched them cross the street and go into the library. Then he noticed that the police car was still running. "Officer—" he stopped. He knew how to turn a key, after all. He got in behind the wheel and turned off the car. Someday soon, he'd be driving. He got out of the car and shut the door then walked to the nearest house where no one had shoveled yet.

Kelly knew that there would be faces in the windows of the neighbors' houses; the lights from the state police car would have caught everyone's attention. She straightened. "I'm okay," she assured Troy. "I'm just shaken a little bit."

"I know. He doesn't have any identification on him, so we have to try to find out who he is. If he comes to the library, you'll know him. It's—we have to do it this way."

"I know."

She walked beside Troy, looking straight ahead, avoiding the faces looking out from their windows. When they went inside the library, Trooper Callahan was standing by the body and the lights in the library were on, dispelling the shadows.

"Mrs. Kennedy," Trooper Callahan said formally, even though they knew each other as Susan and Kelly when they bowled, "I'm sorry to ask you to help us, but we need to know who this person is and if he's familiar to you, it'll save us time in the investigation."

"I know. I understand."

The body was on a stretcher, no longer on the floor. She walked closer to it, uncomfortably aware of the presence of the others: Hayden Croft, known to her but not well, as he was so new to the force; Trooper

Callahan, sober-faced as she always was when in uniform; the other members of the crime unit who had, she knew, taken photographs of the man where he had been found, making their preliminary assessments directly from the crime scene.

That the library would be a crime scene . . .

One of the men watched as she approached the stretcher, and then pulled the sheet down from the face. "Is this person someone you recognize from the library? Someone who came here regularly, or even occasionally?"

She shook her head. It was a man with a brown beard and brown hair, his face empty of expression or emotion. "I've never seen him," she said, relief coursing through her that this man was a stranger.

"Are you sure?" the man pressed. "Is he someone who might have come into the library at some time—"

"Ed, she can't identify every person who comes in. People come in for tax forms, they come in to use the computers, to read newspapers . . . there isn't always interaction," Troy interjected.

"You know we have to make sure," the man, Ed, replied.

"It's okay," Kelly said quickly. "It's . . . I really don't recognize him."

"Okay, she doesn't recognize him," Troy said firmly.

Ed covered the man's face again and signaled to two other men, who came and picked up the stretcher.

"Thank you, Mrs. Kennedy," he said formally. "I'm sorry that we had to bother you."

"You didn't bother me," she said. "This is murder—"

"I'm afraid so. We'll be in here for a few days, checking everything. I understand that the library is closed this weekend anyway. We'll work as quickly and efficiently as we can, but I can't guarantee that we'll be done after Presidents' Day. If we're not, the library will need to stay closed until we're finished."

"I understand."

"The press will be calling," he said. "I hope we can count on you not to say anything. We'll have a statement later today, but until we've done the autopsy and the body has been examined, we don't know anything."

And neither do you, Kelly realized that he was telling her. Politely but firmly.

"I'll take you home," Troy said.

"No, you have work to do," Kelly said. "Where's Arlo? I'll walk home with him."

"You're not walking home and it's not the first time Arlo has ridden in the back of the squad car," Troy said.

"Where is Arlo?"

"In your office," Troy said. "I put him in there so he wouldn't get in the way."

When Kelly opened the door to her office, Arlo was poised and waiting. Kelly buried her hands in his thick fur, finding comfort in the dog's reliable, incontrovertible, reassuring *dogness*. "Hello, Arlo," she said to him. "Let's go home."

11

THE NEWS SPREADS

Kelly was glad that she'd started the soup earlier that morning, and that the bread she'd put out to rise was ready for the next phase of preparation. She wasn't sure that she'd have been able to organize herself to do those simple tasks now. It was odd to feel so tired, she thought, after she'd finished in the kitchen and sank down upon the living room couch, Arlo at her side, his head on her knee, watching her as if he were concerned for her wellbeing.

She petted him and tried to halt the army of thoughts from marching back and forth in her brain, again and again. *The feet of the man, pointing down . . . Arlo wary and sensing that something was not right . . . the procession of law enforcement vehicles, all the people that it took to determine that a crime had been committed*

94

and to examine the library to find clues. The library, now a place where a piece of fabric from the man's clothing, or a hair that didn't belong to him but could just as likely belong to an innocent patron, or mud from the man's shoes . . .

The library. That section of the library, where the romance collection was housed, was now a crime scene. Those shelves, so eagerly and ardently visited by the women whose favorite authors spun tales of passion and desire and affection and fidelity . . . she remembered the discussion she'd had with one of the volunteers, who was annoyed that *Gone with the Wind* was shelved with the historical fiction and not the romance. "It's the greatest romance in American literature," Mrs. Lasslo had insisted. "It belongs here." In vain had Kelly explained that it was a novel about the Civil War, and thus it belonged with others like it, stories which had a context that was historical. Mrs. Lasslo had never conceded the point. Fairly often, Kelly would be shelving books and she'd find *Gone with the Wind* where it didn't belong. She knew the culprit was Mrs. Lasslo, but she never brought the subject up, even though Carmela made a point of checking the section after Mrs. Lasslo had been to the library.

Those were the sorts of things that Kelly loved about the library and her work. People took their books seriously. They loved the stories, they cherished the characters, they came to the library to get books that enriched their imaginations. The library was a community. And now, something out of one of the books on its shelves had suddenly, grotesquely, taken place inside.

And the community would never be the same.

She needed something to do, something physical that would keep her busy and perhaps, keep her mind from circling around and around the image of those shod feet pointing to the floor. She looked out the living room window. The snow had not stopped falling, and there was enough on the sidewalks to justify shoveling it again, regardless of whether Troy or Lucas wanted her to do so. She was in the process of putting on her coat when her phone rang.

"Kelly, it's Sarah. What's going on at the library?"

Belatedly, Kelly realized that she should have contacted the members of the Library Board to let them know what had happened. Sarah Duso had been elected as president of the library board after Mrs. Stark had been arrested for her involvement in the drug trade in Settler Springs. Sarah was a strong library advocate and a fervent supporter of the staff, and she should have been notified.

"I'm sorry, Sarah—there's—the police are there—"

"Kelly, are you crying?"

"No, I—" but she was crying, she realized; tears were trickling down her cheek and her voice was choked with an emotion that she couldn't identify. It wasn't grief, how could it be? She didn't know the dead man. "I'm just—I'm sorry. I should have called you."

"Yes," Sarah said forthrightly. "You should have. I heard about it from Nadia, who heard about it from —well, you know how the town gossip grapevine runs. You were there?"

"Not when it happened. I came in to check the book drop and see if everything was okay, like I always do when we're closed due to weather. Lucas had shoveled, he always does—"

"What's this about him trying to steal the police car?'

"What? Lucas? He wouldn't steal the police car, he doesn't even drive yet."

"Someone saw him get in the driver's side."

"I don't know—but he wouldn't steal a car, any car, but certainly not a police car."

Sarah sighed. "I suppose that's just one of the rumors that's circulating. If there's a Krymanski in the neighborhood, he must be breaking the law. Okay, you went into the library. What happened next?'

Kelly forced herself to calm down as she relayed what had happened, what she'd seen, and that she hadn't recognized the dead man.

"You aren't hurt?"

"No, there was nothing . . . I was just waiting outside while the police came, and the coroner . . . they said the library is a crime scene. They might not be done with their investigation of the—of the crime scene by Tuesday."

"There's nothing we can do about that," Sarah said. "It's a long weekend anyway. Even when they are done, the library is going to be a hot spot. Maybe we should close for all of next week."

"No! I mean—no, I'd rather we don't. I want us to get back to normal."

"It'll be awhile before that happens, Kelly, if an unidentified dead man was found in the library. Was he—is there a lot of blood that has to be cleaned?"

To her surprise, Kelly realized that she couldn't answer that question. "I don't know. I only saw his feet. If there was . . . blood or anything, it would have been at the other end."

"We'll have to find out if any blood got on the books," Sarah said briskly. "I imagine our insurance will cover the replacement costs. Cleaning, that's something else. I don't suppose we're going to be allowed in until they're finished with that part of the investigation. I'll call Brady and let him know that we might have a claim, we're waiting for more information."

"He probably already knows," Kelly said, feeling guilty because she should have thought to call him too. "His aunt lives up the block from the library. I'm sure she saw all the cars and she probably called him."

"Probably. I'd never want to commit a crime in Settler Springs; everyone knows everybody. Listen, Kelly, you—" Sarah's voice, which could sometimes be strident, softened. "You've had a shock. I know you want everything to go back to normal but we don't know what that will take. If you need some time off—"

"I don't."

Sarah sighed again. "Okay. But take care of yourself. Do you want me to call Carmela?"

"No, I'll call her. I should have thought of that. I just . . . I don't know. It's like I just couldn't think of anything but . . ."

"I understand. I'll let you know if I find out anything, but you're the one who's married to a cop. You'll find out first."

"Maybe. I'll let you know if Troy tells me anything."

Kelly steeled herself to call Carmela, who by now might already know what had happened and would be irked that no one had told her. She would have been even more annoyed if she'd gotten a call from Sarah, rather than Kelly. Kelly knew that Carmela had her own sense of protocol and propriety and that meant that she expected Kelly to inform her when anything of significance happened at the library. There could be few things more significant, Kelly acknowledged, than the discovery of a dead body.

"Carmela, it's Kelly, I—"

"I wondered when you'd get around to calling," Carmela's tone was indignant. "I've heard from three members of my church and two library patrons that there are police cars all over the street in front of the library. And some nonsense about Lucas Krymanski going for a joyride in a police car, but I told Sharon that's just plain baloney. Lucas wouldn't steal a police car."

"No, I don't know where that comes from. He was standing with me while we waited. They were in the library a long time."

"Who was in the library a long time?"

"The state trooper, the coroner . . . the people who photograph the crime scene . . . I was there awhile." That wasn't a lie, she had been there a long time, but she hoped that Carmela assumed that this was why Kelly had failed to call her with the news that a dead body had been found in the library.

"You're lucky that whenever it happened, it was before you got there or you could have been killed too," Carmela stated.

Kelly hadn't thought of that. There was no indication that a struggle had taken place, she realized. The chairs and tables, the books on the shelves, everything was as it had been when she and Carmela had left the library the evening before. But that was odd, surely; murder couldn't be done without some kind of scuffle.

"It was quiet when I got there," she said.

"Where was the body?"

"In the romance section."

"The romance section?" Carmela repeated in disbelief. "Somebody killed a person in the romance section? Who's the woman?"

"It's not a woman, it's a man, but I didn't recognize him. He's not one of our patrons."

"A man? Someone killed a man in the romance section? Then the killer has to be a woman."

"Why do you say that?"

"Because if a man was going to kill somebody in the library, he'd kill him in the mystery section or the westerns, or the adventure . . . men don't read the romances and the chick lit."

It was classic Carmela logic, but all the same, Kelly realized, there was some sense to it. If there hadn't been a fight in the library, then the location of the body might not be random.

"I don't know."

"Troy will know."

"He might not be able to tell me," Kelly said, recognizing that this was a time when Troy might have to adhere to a professional code of silence while the investigation was underway. The fact that the body had been found in the place where Troy's wife worked could hold sway over how much he was allowed to divulge.

"Oh, he'll tell you what he can," Carmela said with confidence. "Murder is what brought you two together."

12

MURDER FOR SUPPER

Troy texted her to let her know he was on his way home. Kelly went to heat up the soup that was waiting in a pan on the stove, and put the bread in the oven to warm it. When Troy came in, he smelled the aromas of supper like a welcome.

Kelly came into the living room as he was removing his coat. "Snow is still falling," he said as he hung the coat on the doorknob to dry. "I'm gonna change."

She nodded.

"You okay, hon?"

Kelly nodded again. "Coffee?"

"Anything warm. It's cold out there."

Troy appeared in almost no time at all wearing jeans and a sweatshirt. He went to Kelly who was ladling soup into bowls and wrapped his arms around her waist.

"How are you?"

"I'm working with hot soup here, and if I spill it on me or you, neither one of us is going to feel too great."

He backed away. "Sit down, I'll get this."

"I can do it. I'm all right, Troy."

He hesitated. Kelly had never spoken to him that way. But then again, Kelly had never encountered a dead body in the library.

"No," he said quietly, "you're not okay."

He squeezed her shoulders and then left her to her ladling while he cut slices of bread from the freshly baked loaf.

Kelly placed the soup bowls in front of their chairs and sat down. "Are you—is everyone—"

"The library is closed. It's a crime scene; we'll be back tomorrow, but for right now, since the weather closed the library anyway, it's not going to inconvenience anyone."

"The doors—how did you lock the doors? I forgot to give you my key!"

"Sarah Duso came by to see if she could help. She couldn't, but she has a key she let me use. She said I could keep it until I didn't need it. Kelly, why are you crying?"

"I can't believe I forgot to give you my key!" Kelly sobbed. "Of course you'd need a key to lock up. I didn't think of that, I didn't think to call Sarah and tell her, I didn't tell Carmela until Sarah reminded me, I just can't think of anything but—"

"Kelly. Look at me."

Had he spoken to her lovingly, she probably would have cried more. But his voice was firm and she did as he bade.

"There isn't a protocol for how to handle yourself after you've found a dead man in your place of work. If Sarah hadn't come by, I'd have come home to use your key to lock up the library while Hayden stayed behind to make sure no one came in. You make it sound like you should treat this the way you do when someone says they can't find a book that's overdue."

"No, that's not how I'm treating this! I just—I don't know what to do!"

Troy rose from his chair and went to Kelly's side. "Come on," he urged, wrapping his arms around her. "You can't do anything. Eventually, there will be questions to answer. The man wasn't familiar to you. There's no identification on him. We have to find out who he is first. Then we have to find out why his body was brought to the library."

"He wasn't killed there?"

Troy shook his head. "He was dead when he was brought there."

"That's why there wasn't any blood, at least that I could see." Kelly's voice, still shaken, sounded slightly more normal.

"That's right, there wasn't any blood. We don't know where he was killed. There's no trace of snow or mud on his shoes, so wherever he was killed, it wasn't outside."

"There wasn't any sign of a fight in the library," Kelly said. "The chairs were in their rightful places, nothing was disturbed."

Troy nodded. "Eat your soup," he said as he released her and returned to his seat. "It'll get cold."

"But why would someone go to the trouble of bringing a dead body into the library? He was—you're sure he was murdered?"

"He was stabbed somewhere else. By the time he was brought to the library, he was already dead. His shirt has bloodstains on it, and there are bloodstains on the inside of his jacket, but not the outside. He wasn't wearing the jacket when he was killed."

"But why the library? And why in the romance section?"

"What?"

"The romance section. That's where he was. Why would someone leave a body there? Carmela says it must mean the killer is a woman, because a man wouldn't do that. What's the matter?'

"We didn't notice that. That he was left in the romance section. I guess maybe we'd have gotten to it, but no one mentioned it."

"Carmela thought of it right away."

"Good going for Carmela," Troy said enthusiastically. There were always puzzle pieces to assemble in a murder investigation, and now, thanks to Carmela's perception, one piece was connected. He was relieved to see that Kelly's thoughts had veered away from what she had seen in the library and were now navigating in an analytical, rather than a visceral, direction. He knew that she would be troubled for some time to come over what had happened and he realized that because of his profession and his military background, he had to make himself remember that she was a civilian, and this was not a standard ordeal for her work routine. He made a mental note to approach Rev. Dal, the minister at First Church, for his insights. He was Kelly's minister, and Troy's too, even if he was still fairly new to church attendance; Rev. Dal had married them in the hospital while Troy was still recovering from his injuries, and he was a good guy with a practical approach to spirituality that Troy appreciated.

"Do you think she's right?"

"That the killer was a woman? I doubt if a woman could have carried the body into the library unless she's a triathlete or something. She'd have to be pretty strong to carry him, not to mention tall. He's a six-footer, and not light. Muscular."

"But would a man leave a body in the romance section?"

"We don't know for sure that the killer left the body in that space for a reason."

"But it's out of the way, really. Wouldn't someone bringing a body leave it in a more convenient spot? Whoever did it had to carry it inside the doors and across the library. If he came from the parking lot, he had to come in and then come down the stairs, and then across the library to the stacks."

"The crime scene crew will be able to tell us what entrance the killer used and how far he traveled, probably. They'll be assessing everything."

"But I didn't see any dirt or mud or footprints when I came in."

"Neither did any of us, but people leave traces they aren't aware of. There's the area rug in front of the circulation desk, the rugs at the entrances . . . we'll also be investigating the clothing the murdered man was wearing to see if we find any traces of anything; even a hair or a speck of blood will give us something."

"How are you going to find out who the murdered man is?"

Troy dipped his spoon into the bowl of soup. Homemade soup was something that he'd never get enough of. He'd grown up on Campbell's canned soup and it wasn't until marriage that he'd discovered how broth and vegetables and meat, cooked in a pan over the stove at just the right heat, with just the right seasonings, could serve as an antidote to the cold winter weather. It also served as a balm against days like this, when the nature of his job didn't just strike him, but against the woman he loved as well.

"Send out bulletins, this man is missing. We'll get a response He doesn't look like a vagrant or a transient. His hair was cut, his nails were clean, clothes not worn out . . . someone will know he's missing."

"But if he's not someone I recognize, and he's not part of the regular library community, then how did he get into the library?"

Troy took a bite of bread and chewed it before answering. He didn't want to conduct an investigation at the dinner table.

"Someone had a key," he said.

Kelly's brown eyes turned into circles. "You mean—whoever brought him into the library is someone we know?"

"Someone who has a key or has access to a key," Troy confirmed.

"But—"

"Susan is going to want a list of everyone who has keys to the library."

"Susan—you mean she's the one who'll be leading the investigation? She'll be asking questions—Troy, she's not investigating me, is she? They don't think I'm a suspect!"

"Not really, no. But they have to cross you off the list, even though it's obvious that you didn't do it."

"I—of course I didn't do it. I walked into the library, it's my job, it's where I work, and I saw the man—I saw his feet, that's all I saw, and I called you."

"I know, Kelly, I know. Susan knows it too. But you know how this works. Everyone who is involved, however peripherally, has to be questioned before being crossed off the list. You've read enough mystery novels," he said, trying to use a light tone to ease her obvious alarm. "Doesn't this happen in those mysteries?"

"I read them, I'm not a character in them!"

Kelly put down her spoon and removed her napkin from her lap. She wasn't hungry anymore.

13

TROOPER CALLAHAN'S QUESTIONS

The state police officer who was such a competitive bowler was a very different person when she was Trooper Callahan. She had declined Kelly's offer of tea or coffee.

"Thank you," she said politely. "I already had coffee this morning. As you know, because of Officer Kennedy's unique circumstances, we'll be handling much of the investigation into the murder."

"Unique circumstances?"

"He's married to you. You're the librarian. The body was found in the library."

"Oh."

They were sitting in the living room. The curtains were open to show the span of the white world

114

outside the window. The snow had stopped, but the weather forecasters had warned that the snow wasn't over. The winds were picking up and the temperature was falling. It was going to be, the local meteorologists had observed, one of the coldest Valentine's Day temperatures recorded. Kelly had not expected to spend her first Valentine's Day as Mrs. Troy Kennedy being interrogated by a state policewoman.

"You didn't recognize the man?"

"No," Kelly said, wondering if Trooper Callahan thought she was lying. Why was she asking her this when Kelly had already told her that the man was unfamiliar to her.

"You're sure. He would have looked different."

"You mean, because he would have been alive," Kelly said sarcastically. She apologized immediately. "I'm sorry, I didn't mean to sound like that. I just—I don't know who he was, and I don't understand why someone would leave a dead man in the library."

"We don't understand that either, Mrs. Kennedy," Trooper Callahan said. "It's natural that you would be upset. That's a place you're in every day."

"Our board president wanted to know about—about cleaning it. I didn't notice anything . . ."

"There isn't any blood. Our techs are going over it now. They'll be going over the entire library, but of course, with a public place, there will be traces of a number of people who most likely had nothing to do with the murder. We have to follow up on clues that seem to point to evidence."

"Yes, I understand."

Silence. Trooper Callahan's impassive brown eyes gave away nothing as she studied Kelly.

"You're sure you don't want coffee, or something to drink? It's cold out there." Kelly said, feeling that she was inhospitable if she didn't offer again.

"I'm fine, thank you. But go ahead if you want something."

Kelly shook her head. She didn't. She just wanted this to be over. "No, I'm fine. I just . . . I don't know what I can tell you."

"You can tell me who has a key to the library."

"That's almost impossible to say. When I was hired, I started a key log. Board members, staff, cleaning people, the interlibrary loan driver, they all have keys. But the people who had keys before I came probably still have them. And if someone is doing a program at the library, we'll lend them a key in case they need to go in to set up."

"Do you have the list of people who are known to have keys?"

"It's at the library, in my desk drawer."

"Which drawer?"

Kelly was startled to think that someone, even a police officer, would go into her desk. "The bottom drawer on the left. I can go and get it for you."

"There's no need for you to go to the library right now," Trooper Callahan said. "I'll ask Officer Kennedy to get it when I go back. So what you're saying is that there are a number of people who have keys, and who've had them for some time, and another group who may have keys from the past, but you don't know who they are."

"Yes—it's never been an issue. No one was very comfortable about asking former board members to return their keys."

"Why not?"

"Some of them are library benefactors and donors and the board felt that they'd be offended if they were asked to return the keys."

"Do they go into the library during closed hours?"

"No—I mean, not that I know of, but probably not. Most of the ones I know come in when we're open."

"But if they still have a key, they could come in."

"They could, but . . ."

"We'll need a list of former board members, Mrs. Kennedy. And anyone else who might have had a key from past years. The list in your desk will tell us who has a key now, and a legitimate reason to have one. After I see the list, I'll need to go over it with you so that you can tell me what you know about that person."

"You think one of them is a killer?" Kelly kept her voice even, but it was difficult to do so. Trying to imagine Sarah Duso, the board president, or Ivan Gelnick, the interlibrary loan van driver who dropped off books every Tuesday and Friday, or Jessie and Greg, the cleaning couple, or Chloe or Carmela, or anyone, as a killer was just too incredible to even consider. These were ordinary people who lived in a small town and were known to their neighbors. They weren't killers.

"Have there been any unusual incidents at the library? Any disturbances, or arguments among people in the library?"

Kelly shook her head. "No, we have regulars who come in, sometimes every day to read the newspaper or magazines or use the computers if they don't have their own."

"Nothing out of the ordinary?'

"No. There are people who come in to get the tax forms from the rack. We don't necessarily know who they are."

"Strangers?"

"I wouldn't call them strangers. They're just people we don't usually see."

"Usually see?"

"Or that we've never seen," Kelly corrected herself, realizing that Trooper Callahan expected precise answers to her queries. "But that's—they're coming in for a 1099 or a 1040EZ, they're not coming in to figure out where's the best place to leave a dead body!"

Trooper Callahan remained silent. Kelly wondered if the stoic officer was giving her time to compose herself.

"I'm sorry," she said again. "I'm just finding it hard to think that I might know someone who killed a person and left the body in the library."

"You're not unfamiliar with murder."

"What?"

"Settler Springs has had its share of murders. You were familiar with some of the victims."

"Yes, but I didn't kill them! A lot of it was because of the Starks, you know that. Troy and I, we—I didn't kill anyone!"

There was a brief pause. "No, Mrs. Kennedy, I don't think you did. But we have to investigate every possible lead and you could be connected to someone who did this or knows someone who did this. We can't leave anything to chance. Whoever left the body in the library was someone familiar with the library. It's up to us to find out what the connection is and in order to do that, I need to know what you know about the people who come into the library. This must be very difficult for you, Mrs. Kennedy; murder is never something to take lightly.

We're going to be in there for the next few days, and we can pick up clues from fibers and fingerprints, but as I said before, it's a public place. In order to solve this, we need to have your assistance."

"Of course I'll assist in any way I can—do you know when we'll be able to open again?"

"You're already closed on Monday for the holiday, I understand," Trooper Callahan said. "I spoke with your board president. She is in favor of closing for next week."

"Yes, but I don't know if that's wise. The longer we're closed, the more likely people are to speculate. People will think about the people they've seen in the library and the smallest detail could suddenly seem incriminating. I want us to get back to normal as fast as we can."

"Mrs. Kennedy," Trooper Callahan said, a softening in her gaze, "it won't feel normal for some time."

"I want us to go back," Kelly went on as if the officer hadn't spoken. "I want to get in there, after you're finished, with buckets of water and bleach and I want to scrub it clean. The shelves, the floors, everything."

"There's no blood on the floor or the shelves or the stairs. The man was already dead when he was brought in. He had been killed elsewhere."

"I still want to clean everything. Maybe not everything, but that section. I want to take all the books off the shelves and scrub the shelves, I want to mop the floor. . ."

"I understand."

Maybe she did. But probably she didn't, Kelly thought after Trooper Callahan had asked a few more question and then left. She wouldn't understand that Kelly wanted the romance section to return to what it had been before, a place where readers went to find love stories, so that their imaginations could live vicariously through the pages of a book that evoked passion and devotion. She didn't expect the state police officer to understand. It wasn't her job to understand. But it was Kelly's job as a librarian to make sure that the patrons who came to the library found in books what, perhaps, they had failed to find in real life.

14

KEY SUSPECTS

Even though he knew Kelly wouldn't mind, Troy felt a twinge of uneasiness opening the drawer to Kelly's desk where, Susan Callahan had told him, he would find the key log. It didn't seem right to invade Kelly's desk as if he had a right to do so, just because he was a police officer. Susan Callahan's assumption that it was less culpable an act because he was Kelly's husband didn't mitigate his discomfort.

"Here it is," he said, extending his hand to give it to the state police officer.

To his surprise, Susan sat down in the chair across from the desk. "I want you to look at the names and tell me what you know about the people who have keys," she said.

"Me? I don't know them. I know some of them, but Kelly is the one who really knows them."

"Your wife is going to instinctively try to protect the people she knows. It's how she is. I don't know if she could conceive of someone she knows being a possible murder suspect. I want to hear what you have to say first. I'll talk to her again before we're done investigating, although I don't think she'll want to talk to me. She wasn't very happy with me."

"Why?"

The officer smiled slightly, the movement of her lips gentling the stern angles of her smooth brown features. "I think she felt that I was accusing her of the murder."

"I wonder why she felt that," Troy said, using a flippant tone to disguise his concern that Kelly had been made uncomfortable during the interrogation. He was aware that nobody liked being questioned by the police, but it was different when the person under interrogation was his wife.

"I mentioned that she'd been connected to several of the Settler Springs murders."

"The Starks were the culprits for those, not Kelly!"

"Yes, I know."

"Were you trying to get a reaction from her? Because, let me tell you, Kelly is about the kindest person you'll ever meet, but she's not a doormat for anyone."

He leaned back in Kelly's chair, picturing her in her office. It was tidy, that was no surprise, for Kelly was an orderly person. Even though she wasn't in the office, there were traces of her everywhere: the long, navy sweater coat that she left at the library in case she felt cold; a pair of flats under the desk; the coffee cup she'd gotten at a library conference sometime in the past; a stack of memorial thank you notes that she'd written out, waiting to mail, her handwriting graceful and neat across the envelope, the chocolate candy bar that he'd found in her desk, the box of cashews on her desk; the painting that someone had done, envisioning what the long-ago, burned library at Alexandria might have looked like . . . her office was a miniature identification station. Even a trace of her scent lingered in the office, a lighter version of the fragrance that he smelled on her pillow in their bed.

"No," Susan agreed. "She's very strong. I can see that."

"Not strong enough to carry a dead man's body into the library," Troy corrected her.

"That's not what I'm saying," Susan told him. "She's tall, and in good health, and I know you two run regularly, but I don't see her as the killer."

"You almost sound like you were adding up the possibilities," Troy said, wary at the direction of the conversation and wondering how Kelly could possibly be considered a suspect.

"It's our job, Troy. Anyone could be the killer; but only one person did it. Although there may have been an accomplice. We don't know that yet."

Before Troy could reply, Susan had moved on to the next item. "You've sent the notices to all the departments, asking if anyone has reported the man missing?"

"I sent them this morning. What are you going to do about the press?"

"Nothing for now. All we know is that a dead body was found in the library."

"There's a local journalist, Doug Iolus. He knows the town pretty well."

"You're suggesting that I talk to him?"

"His paper is a weekly," Troy explained. "Everyone in town reads it,"

"Do you have his number?"

Troy gave her the number. Susan entered it into her cell phone contacts.

"Now," she said, "the names on that list."

Troy went over the names. He recognized the board members, although he didn't know all of them. "You already met Sarah Duso," he said. "She became president this year, but she was on the board before she was an officer."

"She seems direct, organized, composed."

"All of those things." He waited for Susan to say more, but she didn't. She was waiting for him to continue looking at the list.

"Board members, you'll have to ask Kelly about some of these. I've never met Rich Barry; he might be one of the no-show members, every board has a couple. Kim Abernath, she's been ill and hasn't been to the meetings lately; getting chemo treatments for breast cancer. The Sloans, they have a cleaning business and they clean the library every other week. Ivan, he delivers the interlibrary loan books twice a week. He comes from the district center, he usually gets here before the library opens, that's why he has a key—"

"Where's the district center?"

"Kensington City."

"A half hour from here."

"Yeah. This is his first stop on his route."

"Is he from around here?"

"I don't know. Caroline Rancotti—I wonder why she has a key, she's not a board member."

Susan's interest quickened and she leaned forward. "Who is she?"

"She and her husband opened a winery. She did a program, wine and cheese party, here. It was before Christmas. I wasn't there, I was still in the hospital. Kelly had to attend, but I don't think she stayed the whole time," he said, recalling that all of Kelly's free time those weeks had been spent at the hospital, at his bedside. "Maybe that's why Caroline has a key."

"Do people who do programs commonly keep their keys?"

"I doubt it, but you'd have to ask Kelly. Or maybe Caroline forgot to return the key."

"Has she lived here a long time?"

"No, she and Keith moved here last year and they bought St. Cecilia's, an old church that was up for sale after the diocese merged parishes, and renovated it into a winery."

"Where are they from?"

"They moved here from Pittsburgh. They have two daughters and they wanted to raise their kids in a small town, away from the city." Troy started to explain why the Rancottis couldn't possibly be the killers, but then he remembered Susan's admonition that it was their job to consider the potential for a person to be, if not the killer, at least a suspect until proven otherwise. Caroline was petite, but Keith was taller and muscular. Physically, he could have carried a body into the library.

But Troy doubted that Keith had done it. Why would he have done it? Unless he knew the person from the past. If the man was from Pittsburgh, that was possible. But it sure wasn't plausible.

Troy continued down the list. When he was finished, he asked, "Do you want me to interview these people?"

"Can you do it objectively? The people you know? The board members are Kelly's employers. Are they going to resent her husband asking them questions that make it sound like he thinks they might have killed someone?"

"They know what I do for a living."

"Okay, then go through the list and question everyone. But let's wait until we have an estimated time of death so you can ask people where they were at that time, and on Thursday night."

"And in the meantime?"

Trooper Callahan stood up. "It's Valentine's Day," she said. "Go get a box of chocolates and bring it home to your wife."

A slow, pleased smile traveled across Troy's face. "So I get the day off?"

"And the night too. We're going to be busy in the days to come, so make sure you do right by her."

"What about you? What about your husband?"

Trooper Callahan waved a hand. "Charlie and I have been married for thirteen years," she said. "We have kids. We're long past the moonlight and roses stage. But let me tell you, there's a lot to be said for having a pool table in the basement."

"I'll keep that in mind when we've got twelve more years behind us," he said. "Right now, I'm going to do some quick thinking. Just about everything is closed and I'm not even going to try to order flowers to be delivered, not with this snowstorm."

"She'll probably forgive you."

"Probably. But I don't want to need forgiveness on our first Valentine's Day as a married couple."

15

VALENTINE'S DAY AT THE CAFÉ

Compared to a murder, the dilemma of how to make their first Valentine's Day together didn't seem all that important, but Troy wanted to do something that would at least ease some of Kelly's mood. Their original plans to attend the First Responder's Valentine's Day dance had gotten him off the hook in terms of finding an original way to celebrate the lovers' holiday, but the snowstorm and now the murder had wiped away that option.

As he was driving home, he turned onto McKinley Avenue and noticed that the lights were on in The Café, although most of the other businesses along the street remained closed due to the snow. On an impulse, he parked the police car, not an easy task given the high mounds of snow on the street that had been created by the plows as they went through town, and knocked on the restaurant door.

He was happy to see Tia Krymanski coming to open it. "Officer Troy! What are you doing out? Don't tell me you and Kelly went for your Saturday run on the Trail today," she said as she urged him inside and closed the door behind him.

"No, not today. Are you open today?"

"We're thinking about opening up for lunchtime. It's Valentine's Day, after all. I've been baking chocolate cakes all morning and Gus is thawing steaks."

"I'm trying to come up with something for Kelly for Valentine's Day. We were going to go to the dance, but then I had the conference in Harrisburg and the snow . . ."

"And the murder at the library," Tia finished. "Thanks, by the way, for letting Lucas stop by your place to answer questions. I know you couldn't tell him a lot, but he appreciated being allowed to ask. You know there's a rumor going around that he tried to steal the police car," Lucas' mother said indignantly.

"I know. It's stupid. Rumors usually are. Lucas didn't try to steal the car. The car was running, he turned it off. I'm glad he did. He's not in any trouble."

"If there's a Krymanski around, people assume there's trouble," Tia reminded him unnecessarily. "But he's actually been growing up lately. I think that what happened with Carrie jolted him out of being a kid. It's not what I'd have chosen for him, but she's okay now and he's okay. I count my blessings. Now, about Valentine's Day . . . you bring Kelly on down and we'll serve the two of you a Valentine's Day dinner that will outdo any dozen roses you'd have gotten her."

"It's a deal. Count this as my reservation. What time?"

"Whatever time you show up. We'll save a table for you."

Troy thanked her and left the restaurant with some optimism. Things were pretty bleak just now, but he had a wife he loved, and friends in the town that he now called home. He drove through town to check on how people were handling the snow. There were a number of people out shoveling and using snow blowers, and he saw youths walking by, shovels in hand, to make money off the storm. He stopped by the police station to update Haydon on how the investigation was going.

"I'll be home if you need anything," he said.

"I think we've already had the excitement," Haydon said. "Trooper Callahan stopped by here a while ago to see if anything came in from the notices that you sent out. I told her nothing yet. She sure doesn't let any grass grow beneath her feet, does she?"

"She's a good cop."

"I didn't say she wasn't. I just wonder if she ever lightens up."

"I've bowled with her. She bowls to win. Other than that, I couldn't tell you much about her, but she's a lot more professional than what the state police had before. She's tough, but I think we're better off working with her than when Stark and Meigle worked together. If you need me, call," Troy said.

When he got home, Kelly was in the living room. The Weather Channel was on the television, and Kelly didn't appear to be watching it, although she wasn't doing anything else.

She smiled when she saw him. "I'm glad you're home," she told him, stretching out of her position to stand and wrap her arms around him. "Are you going back out?"

Troy shook his head, breathing in the warmth of her, the scent of her shampoo, the sensation of closeness that was as much spiritual as it was physical. "It's Valentine's Day, remember? I'm done for the day."

"Valentine's Day."

"Uh-huh. And here I am, no roses, no chocolates . . . what kind of husband am I?"

"The kind of husband who got home safely in a snowstorm," she answered. "That's my kind of valentine. Are you hungry? I made a grilled cheese sandwich for lunch. Want me to make you one?"

"Not now. I've got dinner reservations for us."

"Dinner reservations? Everything in town is closed."

"Not The Café. They're opening for lunch, and Tia says that if we want a steak dinner, they'll have one for us. She's been baking chocolate cakes all morning, she said."

"I don't know . . . I don't know if I feel like going out."

"Tia's feelings will be hurt if we don't show up," Troy said, knowing that if he presented the offer as a favor to someone else, Kelly was more likely to oblige. "They're opening but they don't know who's going to come out in this weather, and it's getting colder."

"I guess we should, then, if they're expecting us to show up. I'm surprised they're opening. Most people are staying home."

"It's Valentine's Day."

"It's hard to think of that, with everything."

"Was Susan Callahan tough on you?" he asked, brushing the curls away from Kelly's face. Touching her this way, not out of desire or physical need, but simply because he savored the texture of her hair, her skin, was another one of the mysteries of marriage. Lust for a woman, that was something he understood. But reverence, that was still new and awe-inspiring.

"I guess she was just doing her job, but I felt like she was trying to get me to reveal something that would prove that I was the murderer, and I know that's stupid of me to think that way, but I guess I let her get to me."

"It's part of being a cop, getting to people," Troy said as he moved to the couch and urged her down beside him. "She knows you didn't kill the guy."

"What's going on now, or can't you tell me?"

"We don't know the identity of the guy who got killed, we don't know the identity of the killer, we haven't talked to the people who have a key to the library," he answered her patiently. "What would you like to know?"

Kelly surprised herself by laughing. "Okay," she said, nestling closer to him. "Since you don't have anything to tell me, and you don't want a toasted cheese sandwich for a late lunch, I guess I'll go figure out what to wear to dinner tonight."

She chose a green and blue plaid knitted skirt with a blue tunic sweater and black boots. Troy, who was wearing dark trousers and a cream colored sweater, raised his eyebrows appreciatively as she walked down the stairs.

"You make stairs look like a runway," he said as he held out her coat.

Kelly smiled. "And you," she said, tapping him playfully on his chest, "are going to talk your way into a batch of homemade brownies tomorrow."

"I sure hope that guy on the turnpike has a girlfriend," Troy remarked as they walked out the door.

"I hope that whoever he is, he found a motel for the night. With the weather turning colder, all the snow that isn't cleared is going to turn to ice. I'm glad you're home safe."

She'd repeated that wish several times since he'd returned early from the conference but every time she said it, Troy was reminded anew of how lucky he was to be married to a woman like Kelly, who treated love the way it should be treated, something precious that needed to be guarded and treasured. He had learned a lot since marrying her, and he knew the learning had just begun.

"Are you sure The Café is open?" Kelly asked when they pulled into a parking space that had been ruggedly created by the previous vehicle.

"Tia said—oh, yeah, look, there are lights—"

"Candlelight? Is that candlelight?"

Troy opened his door. "Wait, I'll open the door. If this is a candlelight dinner inside, then I'd better do things right outside."

He held open the door so that Kelly could get out, then took her arm. She smiled up at him, already willing to fall under the spell of whatever The Café was featuring in the way of ambience.

Just as they approached the door, it opened. Lucas, wearing a white shirt, black trousers, and a tie, met them.

"Lucas?"

"Mom's idea," he said in disgust.

"What's going on?"

"They decided to open the place up for Valentine's Day," he said. "Mom said to keep your booth open for you."

They knew the way to the booth they always sat in when they came in for breakfast after their Saturday morning run at the Trail, but the restaurant had been transformed by the candlelight into a mysterious place. There were candles everywhere, wreathing the other diners in shadows that preserved privacy for couples. Troy noticed several heads looking up as he entered, but he couldn't discern anyone's features and he doubted if anyone could tell who he was either, although with Kelly's red hair, he supposed they'd figure it out.

"There's only one thing on the menu," Lucas said after they were seated. "Steak oh pover."

"Steak—oh, yes," Kelly said. "That sounds perfect."

"Your choice of vegetable," Lucas continued doggedly. It was apparent that he'd memorized the Valentine's Day special. "Broccoli with hollandaise sauce or champignons—those are just mushrooms with some kind of sauce or something on them," he said in a low voice. "And a baked potato," he finished on a note of triumph with a familiar menu item, "because Mom says French food isn't very filling. And for dessert, there's something that Mom calls a ganache, but it's really just chocolate cake. It's real good, though, I had some."

"Thank you, Lucas," Troy said soberly, hoping that the dim candlelight would conceal his amusement. "I think you have the makings of an excellent waiter."

"No thanks," Lucas said. "Mom made me do this. I had to quit doing snow shoveling so I could get dressed for tonight and practice saying the menu."

"There will still be snow tomorrow," Kelly said.

"It's too hard to shovel after it freezes," he complained. "I tried to tell Mom but she wouldn't listen."

"I think you might make up the difference in tips tonight," Troy suggested.

Lucas brightened. "Yeah, I've gotten a good stash so far," he said. "I'll let Mom know you're here so that she can cook your food."

After he left, Kelly reached her hand out and placed it on top of Troy's hand. "Thanks," she said.

"For the comic relief?" he asked. "I didn't know that was included in the Valentine's Day menu."

"For that, and for this, and for everything," she said earnestly.

Her eyes gleamed in the candlelight, which flickered against the gold necklace at her throat. "I haven't been handling everything well and it's not your fault, or even Trooper Callahan's fault, that this happened. I'm acting like it happened to me because it happened at the library and that's selfish. The library doesn't belong to me. That poor man who was killed . . . it wasn't his fault that he was left in the library. I want you to find out who did this, and I'll do whatever I can to help you with that."

16
THE CRIME-SOLVING STAFF

The library wasn't ready to open yet, but Kelly, Carmela and Chloe had gone in as soon as the police and crime scene experts had given their permission. Both staff members agreed with Kelly that, even if there were no traces of evidence from the crime, they wanted to give the library a thorough cleaning.

"All the books in the romance section off the shelves," Kelly said. "The shelves scoured with detergent. The floors mopped. I don't know when Greg is going to come back from Tennessee; he left a message on the machine that he's been delayed because of the snow and I don't want him to feel like he has to hurry back. We'll explain what happened when he returns. In the meantime, I think we can take care of this."

So they came to work in jeans and sweatshirts and sneakers and decided to give the entire library, not just the romance section, a thorough going over. Every time the telephone rang, Kelly grew tense; Sarah had said that the staff was to refer any questions about the murder to her. It was a reasonable decision; the library board didn't want the staff to be bothered by members of the press, and the police didn't want details leaking out. All the media knew was that the body of a murdered man had been found in the library, probably left there sometime between the library's closing time on Thursday and Friday morning. He had been killed elsewhere and his body brought to the library. The cause of death was stabbing. Police were exploring the town and the nearby area to discover where he had been killed. There were no suspects as of yet.

There wasn't much to leak out, from the little that Kelly knew. The police were still waiting to learn the identity of the murdered man. Questioning of the people who had keys to the library had yielded plausible alibis from those who had been interrogated. All said they had been home that night because of the snow. Kelly had put together a list of former board members who might still have keys, and Troy had questioned them, but none of them had a key anymore, or admitted to having one, and they all said that they hadn't gone out that night of the storm.

Susan Rancotti, when asked why she hadn't returned her key after the program, had told the police that she just forgot. She was at first horrified, and then offended, to think that this made her a possible suspect, especially when her husband vouched for the fact that they had both been home that evening. They had been alone because Caroline's parents had taken the kids for the long weekend, by prior arrangement because Caroline and Keith had been scheduled to serve their wines at the First Responders' Valentine's Day dance. The dance had been cancelled, but by then, Keith had told Trooper Callahan, the kids were already at their grandparents and he and Caroline decided that they'd stay at home and enjoy the time together.

Kelly was fearful that Caroline would carry a grudge if she felt that the library had offered her up as a suspect to the police and wanted to talk to her, but Sarah had advised against it. Right now, with a murder investigation going on, she had told Kelly, it was better to say no more than what needed to be said. The police were checking every angle and they'd find out on their own if there was any reason to suspect the Rancottis of the murder.

Kelly didn't like that advice but she couldn't flout the board president's instructions. It was practical and logical, just as Sarah herself was, but it wasn't the way that Kelly liked to handle matters with library supporters. Sarah had even told her not to talk with Doug Iolus about the murder, even though he was a friend and not just the journalist who covered the town and gave the library excellent publicity when activities were scheduled.

There was much to think about, and Kelly had often found that administering what her grandmother had called "a good thrashing to dirt" was an excellent way to expel the doubts and clouds of worry that obstructed her thinking. Each of the women took a book cart, a sponge, and a pail of water to the areas they were going to clean, setting off as if they were warriors. Each one, in a different way, keenly felt the desecration that had been visited upon the library by the murder, and even though it had not taken place in the library, it had ended here. Chloe had wanted to invite a friend of hers to do a spiritual cleansing, to which Camila had snorted with the affirmation that if bleach couldn't cleanse, nothing could. Kelly kept the peace between the two opposing points of view, but decided that some sort of recognition of the tragedy would be necessary. The form that it would take remained to be decided.

Shelf by shelf, she removed the books from their position, placing them on the cart while she washed the shelf clean, then dried it thoroughly and left it bare before returning the books to their spot. Along the way, of course, she found books that were out of order and she reshelved them correctly.

There was no reminder in the romance section that this had been a resting place for a dead man, nor was there any blood to indicate that a murder had preceded the placing of the body on the floor. Still, Kelly's imagination could not help but instinctively recoil whenever she spotted something that looked like blood, even if it was only part of the color scheme of a book spine, or a bookmark that someone had left.

She was cleaning the shelf which contained the books of one of the most popular of the romance writers—a novelist whose works were enjoyed by readers, mostly women, of all ages for the sensitive and honest way they dealt with the trials of people in love—when she saw something glinting in the metal track where the books had been before she put them on the cart. It was a ring, a simple gold wedding band, a woman's ring, to judge from the size.

If someone had lost a wedding ring, that person would certainly have let the library staff know. But no one would lose a ring behind the books; patrons pulled books off the shelves when choosing them, they didn't remove the whole author section. Kelly wasn't sure what to do, but taking a tissue, she wrapped the ring inside it and put it in her desk drawer. It seemed as if it might be important, something she would mention to Troy, for his thoughts. If he agreed, he would tell Trooper Callahan. Despite her realization that the impassive state police officer had a job to do and could not allow sentiment to interfere, Kelly did not feel comfortable approaching the woman with a discovery that could just as easily be discounted as irrelevant.

The discovery of the dead man's body seemed to have opened Kelly's eyes to other epiphanies, equally unwelcome. She had formerly thought of Susan Callahan as a friend, a fellow bowler on the First Responders' bowling team, someone whose company she had enjoyed in a relaxed, casual atmosphere. Now, coming up against the officer's professional side, Kelly was no longer sure that she knew the woman at all. Another casualty of the murder was the forthright manner in which board president Sarah Duso had claimed authority. Kelly had been used to near autonomy in library matters, except during the unpleasant time when Lois Stark had sought to inflict her control over the staff and library operations to suit her own selfish ends. This was not Sarah's motive, Kelly knew. But acclimating to an assertive board president was yet another reminder that the new year had brought changes that were not easily accepted.

It was nearly lunchtime. Kelly removed her rubber gloves and left them on the cart. She was on her way to the library restroom to wash her hands when the silence of the library was interrupted by Chloe, calling out over the balcony.

"Kelly, Carmela, come up here!"

Carmela groaned audibly. "What is it?" she demanded. She too, was on her way to wash her hands and take her lunch break and was in no mood for what she regarded as Chloe's melodrama.

"Come up here!" the young librarian student insisted.

Kelly was taller and younger and she moved faster than Carmela, who was in no hurry to encourage Chloe's flair for theatrical announcements.

When they reached the Children's Corner, Chloe was standing by the display stand where representations of famous children's literary characters were posed. Kelly's gaze quickly swept over Raggedy Ann, to make certain that she wasn't wearing a bikini again, but the red-headed rag doll was attired in her usual dress and pinafore.

"What is it?" Carmela demanded.

Chloe pointed to a set of ceramic figures from *Peter Pan*: Peter, Wendy and her brothers, Captain Hook, Tiger Lily, Tinker Bell, and the crocodile.

"What is it?" Carmela repeated. "They're all there."

"Look at Tinker Bell!"

The women went closer and saw what it was that had caught Chloe's notice. Encircling the miniature figurine of the diminutive Tinker Bell was a diamond ring.

THE SEVENTH COMMANDMENT

"**S**omeone lost a ring," Carmela said. "Put it in a plastic bag and lock it in the money box and we'll try to find out who might have lost it. It's not much of a diamond," she commented.

"It's probably an engagement ring," Chloe protested.

"This is a funny place to lose an engagement ring."

"Don't touch it," Kelly said as Chloe reached out to take the ring. "Here," she took a tissue from the pocket of her jeans. "Pick it up with this."

"You think it's a clue?" Chloe asked breathlessly.

"I don't know, but I found a wedding ring just a few minutes ago in the romance section shelves. It seems a little strange that two rings would be lost in the library in two different places."

"Where did you find it?" Carmela asked.

"In the romance section—"

"No, where? By what book?"

"One of Priscilla Tobin's books," Kelly said. Then she suddenly realized why Carmela was pressing the matter. "You think the author might have been deliberately chosen?"

"If there was ever a hussy in children's literature it's Tinker Bell," Carmela answered bluntly. "Which book was the ring closest to?"

"It was behind—I don't know, I'll have to put the books back the way I took them out, and then I'll know."

"Let's take care of that now," Carmela said. "It might tell us something."

The three women, even Carmela, wasted no time in hurrying down the stairs to the romance section. Testing first to confirm that the shelf was completely dry, Kelly began to replace the books. "It was here," she said, pointing to the small space in the shelf tracking where she had found the ring."

She put the Tobin books back in their places. The women leaned forward as Kelly began to pull the books away to see which one was in front of the space.

The Seventh Commandment, by Priscilla Tobin.

"Which one is that?" Chloe asked.

"'Thou Shalt Not Commit Adultery'" Carmela recited from memory, too absorbed in the meaning of the placement of the ring to chide Chloe for her ignorance.

"Adultery."

"And an engagement ring is a promise," Chloe said.

"Putting it by Tinker Bell might have been deliberate."

"It might also have nothing to do with the murder," Kelly said realistically.

"You don't believe that," Carmela challenged her. "You know there was a connection."

"I think there is," Kelly admitted, "but I don't know if the police will."

"You're married to Troy. He'll listen to you."

"He'll listen but he can't base an investigation on it. Let's go sit down and eat our lunches and see what we can come up with. I'd like us all to mull this over before I bring anything up to Troy, so that if he does think it's worth following up on, he can make a good case for it to Trooper Callahan."

"She scares me," Chloe admitted as they were sitting down at one of the tables, their lunches in front of them and the coffee carafe in the middle. "I felt like I was a suspect, all because I have a key to the library. Of course I have a key, I work here. But when I told her that I sometimes come in when no one is here, so I can set up for a kids' program or decorate, I felt like she had me under a microscope."

"She brought up me being a suspect in Lyola Knesbit's murder," Carmela, clearly still singed by the episode the year before, brought up. "Even though Travis Shaw has been convicted and sentenced for it, she made me feel like I knew something the police didn't."

"I guess it's just her way," Kelly said, even though she shared the way her co-workers felt after being interrogated by the officer. "I thought the way you did, that she was trying to figure out if I had done it. None of us did it, we know that. But maybe we can figure out some things that the police can't figure out, just because we work here and we'll notice things they wouldn't. Like you realizing that the man's body was left in the romance section,

Carmela," Kelly said. "The police might not have noticed that as fast as you did. Troy said no one noticed it at the time."

Carmela didn't exactly preen at this praise, but there was no mistaking the look of satisfaction on her face.

"I wouldn't expect the police to notice what we do," Chloe said. "This isn't exactly prime turf for a murder investigation. But now that it's happened, I'm wondering what else happened here that we thought was just random."

"Like those wine glasses in the stacks," Kelly recalled suddenly. "Carmela, you remember when you were shelving books and you found them?"

"I remember. It was in the books on marriage and infidelity," Carmela said slowly.

"The Seventh Commandment," Chloe said reverently, struck by the pairing. "We thought the wine glasses were left over from the Rancottis' wine and cheese party—"

"And that still might be the case," Kelly said quickly, her heart sinking as she realized that this might be a clue that pointed, however circumstantially, to Caroline and Keith.

"It might," Carmela nodded, but her expression was dubious. "It's worth telling Troy."

"Do you think . . . what about when my Valentine's Day display was vandalized?" Chloe recalled. "The heart shaped confetti was all over the floor. It was the same time that Raggedy Ann was wearing a bikini top."

"I still think that was just someone playing a prank," Carmela said.

"I'll mention it to Troy," Kelly said. "It's better if he has everything that we know and he can decide what to tell Trooper Callahan."

"I wish we knew who the man was," Chloe said. "Maybe then we'd have a better idea of how to solve this."

"You saw the photograph from the police, and I saw him," Kelly said. "He wasn't familiar to me at all."

"But what if he was a parent of one of the kids who comes to the Children's Corner?" Chloe insisted. "The parents don't always linger. Maybe he came upstairs to get books for a child."

"Then one of us would have recognized him," Carmela said. "I check the books out for patrons, and when I'm at lunch, Kelly does it. He's a stranger."

"Not to someone," Chloe insisted. "Someone knew him, and someone had a reason to kill him and a reason to leave him here. But it doesn't make sense, does it?"

"Why should murder make sense?" Carmela inquired.

"Not that . . . it's like someone was leaving clues in the library. Why would anyone do that?"

"We can't be sure they're clues," Kelly cautioned, although she agreed with Chloe that there was something deliberate in the placing of the rings. "I don't know what else they could be," Kelly admitted.

"You'll tell Troy?"

"I'll definitely tell Troy," Kelly promised. "But this has to stay among the three of us. If it is a clue, it's important that the police are the only ones to have the information. Can we all agree to keep this quiet?"

Chloe seemed caught off guard by the serious tone of Kelly's question. But Carmela, who recalled all too well how quickly speculation turned to belief was nodding emphatically. "Don't say anything," she said. "If it gets out, we'll know, and the police will know too, that it came from here." She fixed a meaningful stare on Chloe, whose eyes widened as if to indicate that she would never have thought to reveal what she knew. But, Kelly knew, it would have been natural for Chloe to tell her friends. Chloe was in her early twenties, enthusiastic and vivacious, and to her, the murder investigation taking place over the discovery of the body in the library was a source of excitement. Had the body been found in the Children's Corner, she might have had a very different reaction.

"Carmela is right," Kelly said, reinforcing what the redoubtable library technician had said. "The police will know and they'll trace the story back to one of us. So it stays here. I'll tell Troy tonight—"

"You shouldn't wait until tonight," Carmela interrupted. "This might be important. You need to tell him now."

"He's on duty—"

"And he's investigating a murder. Tell him now. The sooner they solve this, the sooner we can get back to normal. There's no reason to delay when there's a murder investigation underway."

Carmela was, of course, right. "I don't want to tell him over the phone."

"No, you don't. Chloe and I can keep on cleaning here. You can go over to the station and tell him. Be careful, it's awful icy out there."

The borough crew had done its best to clear the snow from the roads, but so much snow falling in such cold temperatures left the streets precarious. Kelly had walked to work, wearing her sturdy boots to keep her from falling. It was still possible to walk in the snow, which was less likely to lead to a fall, even if it took longer. By the time she had walked the comparatively short distance from the library to the police station, her legs were as tired as if she'd gone running on the Trail.

When she opened the door to the police station, she was taken aback to see that Troy was not alone. Trooper Callahan was in his office and the door was closed.

Chapter Seventeen Clues from the Library

Troy saw her through the glass in the office door and waved her in, standing up as she entered and pulling a chair closer to the desk so that she could sit down.

"Kelly, I didn't know you were coming by. You look like you've been climbing Everest," he said, motioning to the snow that covered the bottom of her coat.

"I figured it would be easier to walk than to drive. I'm less likely to fall in the snow, but the drifts are pretty high. The roads are still icy."

"I know. Leo is trying to get more salt for the crew. We used up most of our allocation this winter; no one expected so much snow, and this last storm has just about depleted us."

Trooper Callahan rose. "I'll get back to you if I get any leads on identification," she said. "Good afternoon, Mrs. Kennedy—"

To her own surprise, Kelly heard herself suggesting that what she had to say might be of interest to both of them. "It might be nothing," she said awkwardly, as the state police officer's unrevealing eyes drilled into her. "But . . ."

"Did something turn up at the library?" Troy asked.

"No, no—I mean yes, but it's nothing that any of your officers would have been likely to find. They already had the knife, so they weren't looking for a murder weapon."

"They were told to search the area," Trooper Callahan said.

"And I'm sure they did, but this . . . this wasn't something that they'd have known to look for. We wouldn't have found anything if we weren't cleaning." Trying to be succinct, she took out the two baggies, each containing a ring, and put it on Troy's desk. "I found the wedding ring in the romance section, behind a Priscilla Tobin novel titled 'The Seventh Commandment.'"

"Adultery," Susan Callahan said.

"Yes. Chloe, our children's librarian, found this diamond ring up in the Children's Corner; it had been placed over a ceramic figurine of Tinker Bell."

"Tinker Bell?" Troy asked. "I don't get it."

"Maybe it's nothing," Kelly said hurriedly. "But we thought it might be something . . . a couple of other things, earlier, probably nothing."

"Go on," Trooper Callahan said, her dark gaze intent on Kelly.

"Well, two weeks or so ago, a little more than that, Carmela was shelving the books and she found wine glasses in the section where the books on marital problems are located. Five books had been taken out and she was putting them back. That's when she found the wine glasses. It's probably from the wine and cheese fundraiser that we had just before Christmas," she said quickly.

"You told me about Carmela finding those glasses," Troy recalled. "It was before the conference in Harrisburg. It didn't sound like anything but sloppy housecleaning at the time."

"Wine and cheese? Who provided the wine?"

Of course Trooper Callahan had caught the wine reference and logically enough, was making her own connections. "The Rancottis," Kelly said.

Trooper Callahan nodded. "When she or her husband checked out these books, did you or anyone else on staff notice the topic?"

"The books weren't checked out through the system," Kelly said. "They were taken out of the library and then put in the book drop, where Carmela found them and shelved them."

"Taken out? During library hours?"

"It's possible. Someone could take out books without us knowing. It's winter, it's easy enough to hide a book inside a coat. There's not a lot of circulation for books in that section."

"Somebody who's having marriage problems might not want people to know about it," Troy said.

"Or somebody with a key to the library came in after hours and took the books out," Trooper Callahan said.

Back to the library key again. Kelly had hoped that the state police officer wouldn't connect those dots.

"We don't really know how the books were taken out," she said. "We just know they were returned."

"I'd better go talk to the Rancottis again," Troy said, sounding grim.

Kelly wanted to protest that Caroline and Keith couldn't possibly have murdered anyone, but she knew that this was not her domain. She could offer advice and insights about books, but she could not dismiss a possible link between a murderer and a motive.

"When was the fundraiser?"

"January. Early January."

"This was a fundraiser. So you have a list of the people who paid to attend?"

Kelly paused. "We should have, but our reservation lists are sometimes a little haphazard. Most of them are library supporters, but there were a few people from the community who were interested in sampling the wines. I can put together the list for you."

The officer nodded. "We're still trying to fill in the hole," she said. "We don't know the identity of the victim and we don't know where he was stabbed to death. The toxicology reports . . ." she paused, then went on. "The toxicology reports show that the victim had ingested a drug that's prescribed for people who have trouble sleeping. A higher dosage than one would typically take. Troy, hold off on the Rancottis until we have more on the victim. After your wife gives you the list, go ahead and talk to the people who attended the wine and cheese fundraiser."

"And notice if any of the married women aren't wearing their rings," Troy said.

Trooper Callahan nodded. "Thank you, Mrs. Kennedy. This could be very helpful."

"Is there a reason why I'm Kelly at the bowling alley and Mrs. Kennedy when you're in uniform?" Kelly asked.

The state police officer looked momentarily surprised before her features composed themselves into her usual stoic expression. "Some people find it easier," she said, "for that dividing line to stay up."

"I'm not one of them," Kelly said. "If I know your first name and you know mine, I'd rather use it than bounce back and forth like we've forgotten who the other one is."

The officer gave a brief nod of her head. "I'll remember that," she agreed. "Troy, keep me informed."

After she left the office, Troy came over to Kelly and hugged her. "You've been busy, you and your library sleuths," he said.

"We weren't really trying to be sleuths, though. We just found these things and thought they might be important."

"I'm sure they are. Especially if no one has reported losing a ring."

"No one has. But Troy, I just don't think that Caroline or Keith did this."

Troy looked troubled. "Maybe they didn't. But right now, they're the closest thing we have to suspects. Does Caroline wear a wedding ring?"

"I don't . . . I never noticed if either one of them does," Kelly acknowledged, thinking back. "But Troy, that doesn't make them killers! Maybe their rings would be stained, working with wine, I don't know! There are people who don't wear rings."

"I know. And that alone doesn't make them guilty. Don't worry, Kelly, no one is going to be accused without cause. It's not Roger Stark running things, you know. Susan is tough, but she's fair. She wants to find the killer, not just accuse someone so she can close the case. I was glad you said that to her, about calling you by your name. I wondered the same thing: why had you suddenly become Mrs. Kennedy when you'd been Kelly for weeks. Try to remember that she's new around here, and she's trying to build a reputation as an honest officer in a department that's had its own scandal lately. Plus, she's a woman. A black woman. She has a number of obstacles in her way as soon as she puts on her uniform."

"I can imagine how hard it must be for her and I don't doubt her integrity. But Caroline and Keith, they're going to be so upset by all of this. They really are good people, I'm sure of it. I don't want them to hold the library responsible for . . . for what might happen."

"It's not really about the library, Kelly," he said to her, his inflection soothing. "I know that you can't help but think of this personally because you care so much about the library and the town. It's one of the things about you that I love the most, the way you don't hold back when someone needs your help. But this time, you have to hold back. You can't get in the way."

It was another reminder, akin to the words of Sarah Duso and Trooper Callahan, that her natural tendency to believe people and to support them was out of place in this investigation. In the past, when she'd helped try to unearth the identity of the criminals who had caused Lucas Krymanski, Carmela Dixon, even Reverend Dal, to be looked at with suspicion because they seemed complicit in a crime, her steadfast loyalty had been an asset. Now, it seemed, it was a detriment, one so fraught with potential to cause problems that even Troy felt the need to caution her against her own nature.

"I'd better get back to the library," she said, buttoning her coat. "I just came by to drop off the rings and tell you what we had found."

"Kelly—"

"We're not done cleaning," she said. "We want everything to be perfect so that we're ready when we're allowed to open back up."

"Kelly, please don't feel like you're doing something wrong," Troy pleaded. "You're not."

"I feel like I am," she said, wrapping her scarf around her neck. "I feel like I'm being scolded and told to stay out of this or I might mess it up. And I know that you're right, you and Susan and Sarah. You're all right. This isn't my job to fix. I do need to stay out of it. I'll try as hard as I can."

He hugged her but she was not pliable in his embrace and he knew that she was more deeply hurt by his words than she had been by the instructions of the board president or the state trooper, because her link with them was professional. He was married to her.

"I'm sorry, Kelly," he said. "I'll—this is new territory for me too. We'll figure out a way to navigate it."

MARRIAGE AND MURDER

Despite his assurance that he and Kelly would find a way to navigate the rocky shoals of this investigation and its overlapping into their personal and professional lives, Troy was unsure how to accomplish this. When he went home, Kelly seemed to be no different than usual. A little quieter, perhaps, a little more thoughtful, but he couldn't be sure if this was because of what he had said or because of the murder itself.

She talked of the cleaning that had been done and the things that they were doing to make sure that the library presented a hospitable appearance when they opened.

"People are going to be curious," he said over dinner. "They might come in just to see where it happened."

"Sarah said that we're to tell them we don't know anything, if they ask," Kelly said. "She says no one will know how much we actually know and they can assume that the only ones who know are the police."

"It's good advice," Troy said. He noticed that Arlo had taken to lying by Kelly's chair of late, as if he sensed that she was troubled and wanted to offer his consolation in his own way. Maybe Arlo would be more successful in providing comfort.

Kelly had put a roast, potatoes and carrots in the crockpot before leaving that morning and by the time he arrived home, the aroma had permeated throughout the house. After the first bite of tender roast, he praised her cooking.

"The crockpot did all the work," she said lightly.

"I didn't marry the crockpot."

She smiled, but he noticed that she looked tired, her usual vivacity subdued. "Kelly, I wish for so many reasons that this hadn't happened," he said. "But since it did, we can't let it put a wedge between us."

"There's no wedge between us," she said. "Sarah doesn't want us to open yet. We've cleaned the library from top to bottom, we've put up displays, we've done everything to make sure that it looks normal. But she wants us to wait. She says there's no point in opening for one day before we close for Sunday anyway."

"It's not going to be pleasant when you do open," Troy warned her. "Even the regular patrons are going to want to talk about it to you."

"I don't want to talk about it."

"I know you don't. But they'll ask. By now, everyone knows that you found the body. People are going to ask."

"I'm not going to answer."

"No, you don't have to answer. But you have to know what you're going to say. And then you give that same answer to everyone who asks. It doesn't matter if it's "I called the police and left the library as soon as I saw the body; I didn't recognize the victim; I have nothing to add" or "I've been advised by my attorney to say nothing—"

"My attorney! I don't have an attorney! I don't need one, I didn't kill the person—"

Troy spread out his hands in a gesture of pacification. "I know that. I'm just trying to think of things that you can say when people ask you. Or," he said, thinking aloud, "you can stay in your office, close the door and let Carmela handle them. She's not likely to welcome any questions. She remembers what it felt like to be a suspect. Of course," he went on, returning his attention to the meal that richly deserved it, "you may not have any patrons at all coming in after they've been treated to the rough side of Carmela's tongue if they have questions to ask."

That brought a smile, a genuine smile, to Kelly's features. "That's true," she admitted. "I can guess how she'll react. But I might just do that. For the first few days, anyway. Carmela won't mind."

"Just make sure that you know what to say and what not to say."

"I already know that, Troy," Kelly replied wearily. "Susan Callahan already stopped by to give us the lecture. And Sarah is coming in tomorrow to talk to us. I'm starting to wonder if she wants to be the voice of the library response because she likes the attention."

"Do you really think that?"

"I don't know. She said that we're to refer all press questions to her."

"Maybe she's just trying to spare you and Carmela and Chloe from having to answer uncomfortable questions."

"I feel like we're being treated like children. We know the library and our patrons better than anyone else could."

"I don't see how Sarah would benefit from the attention," Troy noted.

Kelly sighed. "I know. I hate all of this. It has me looking askance at everyone who's connected to the library."

"What you're really annoyed at," Troy said, "is that she's not letting you make things right with the Rancottis."

Kelly didn't deny this. "It doesn't help the library if Caroline thinks that we believe she and Keith killed this man," she said.

Troy didn't bother to say that if the Rancottis were the killers, they'd be in no position to support the library from a prison cell. Nor did he decide to tell Kelly that he was going to be speaking to the Rancottis again. The police still had no identification on the murder victim and as a result, they had no choice but to go back over their list of potential suspects. It was a short list and not a very convincing one.

Troy didn't tell Kelly that he'd be talking to Caroline and Keith Rancotti, but by the next afternoon, she knew. The library was still closed to patrons, but the staff continued to go in according to schedule to work on various projects. Kelly was reviewing the library mailing list in preparation for the annual "I Love My Library" solicitation campaign when she heard a pounding on the front glass doors of the library. Looking up, she saw Caroline Rancotti out front.

"That's trouble," Carmela predicted.

"I can't ignore her," Kelly said as she left the table where she was working and went to the door.

Unlocking the door, she moved back so that Caroline could enter. It was apparent that Caroline was in a temper. Her hair was tousled from the wind, her coat was unbuttoned, and her eyes were blazing.

"I can't believe that, after we tried to help the library, you would turn on us like this!"

"Turn on you? Caroline, I haven't done that. I don't know—"

"I suppose you don't know that your husband came to our place of business—our winery, our place of business—to 'talk' to us. Again. I suppose you don't know—"

"No, Caroline," Kelly said, holding onto patience because she could understand why Caroline was upset, even though Kelly had had nothing to do with Troy's interrogation. "I don't know. If Troy went to talk to you, he didn't tell me about it. He knows that I don't believe you and Keith did this."

Caroline, who had been drawing in breath for the next outburst, suddenly seemed to deflate. "You don't?" she said, her shoulders sagging. "You don't think we're guilty?"

"Of course I don't! Why would I?"

"But who told them that we had a key? Here!" Caroline took the library key from her pocket and handed it to Kelly. "I wish we'd never done the fundraiser. We'll never do another one for the library, I can promise you that much!"

"Caroline, look, I don't believe you and Keith had anything to do with the murder. The police are investigating, they have to. They're interviewing everyone who has a key to the library. They've interviewed all three of us."

"But you work here. They expect you to have keys. They think we kept the key so we could hide a body here! It's ridiculous! How could we possibly murder a person, hide the evidence, and then bring the body here? Why would anyone do that? If someone kills someone, why would they bring the body to a place where it's sure to be found?"

"I don't know, Caroline. I don't understand any of this. I just wish they'd identify the victim, find out who killed him, and let us all go back to the way things were."

"They'll never be the way they were! Keith and I want to sell the winery and move," Caroline declared. "We want to get away from this hateful, horrible place where people pretend to be your friends and then, just because we're strangers and new to the town, they decide that we must be guilty. You should have stuck up for us, Kelly. You're as much to blame as anyone for this. You let us think we had a place here, and—"

"Hold on!" Carmela came forward. "Kelly isn't to blame for this. The killer is to blame. How do you think we like it? Someone had a reason for bringing that body to the library and we don't know who it was. We don't know if it was someone we know, someone who uses the library regularly. We like to think we know all our patrons, but there's a stranger among us. I don't think it's you any more than Kelly does. But it's someone, and we need to find out who. Moving from Settler Springs won't help the situation. Finding out who did this will."

"I don't know who did it and it doesn't appear that the police do either!" Caroline flared back. "It appears that your yokel police force is entirely incompetent."

"Troy isn't incompetent!" Kelly said angrily. "Solving a murder in real life isn't the same as reading a mystery novel. It's a lot of tedious work. They've sent out photographs, descriptions, and there's still no response on this man's identity. How can someone disappear and no one notice?"

"Well, he's certainly not a local. In this town, everyone minds everyone else's business! You'll all protect the real killer because he's one of you and you'll let newcomers like me and Keith take the blame for something we didn't do!"

BRINGING WORK HOME

Despite Carmela's insistence, after Caroline's irate departure, that she was wrong about the library and wrong about the town, that accusation continued to resound in Kelly's thoughts as she returned to work and later, after she returned home.

She was surprised to find Troy already home when she arrived home. The front sidewalk and steps had been freshly shoveled and salted, his Suburban was in the driveway, and his coat was in the closet. She took off her coat and boots and padded in her stocking feet to the kitchen, where she found Troy, standing over the stove and muttering over a frying pan.

"You're home early," she said, leaning over his shoulder to peer into the pan, where sausages, chopped green peppers and onions were sizzling.

"I thought I'd give you a break," he said, wrapping one arm around her waist while he continued to stir at the contents of the frying pan with the spatula in his other hand. "Potatoes are baking in the oven and there's a salad in the fridge."

"Very nice," she said, breathing in the aroma of cooking food appreciatively. "What brings you home so early?"

"Dead ends," he admitted frankly as he put two plates on the table. "We're just not gaining any traction. How can a guy completely disappear and no one notice he's gone? How can so many people have keys to the library and airtight alibis?"

"The Rancottis?" she asked quietly, placing silverware by the plates.

Troy turned; there was a note in her voice that alerted him that something was wrong.

"I went to see them today," he answered guardedly.

"I know. Caroline came to the library." Kelly opened the refrigerator and took out the bowl of salad and the bottles of dressing; ranch dressing for Troy, Italian for her.

Troy couldn't read her expression because she was moving around the kitchen, doing the ordinary tasks in preparation for the meal, yet he couldn't help feeling that she was deliberately avoiding his gaze.

"She did? Why?"

"She's upset. She thinks we're throwing her to the wolves."

"You aren't throwing her to anyone," Troy replied, his tone harsh. "She and Keith are being questioned just like everyone else who has a key to the library. She had no reason to go running to you."

"She thinks it's because—you'd better check the sausages," Kelly said, "it sounds like they're cooking fast."

Troy muttered an oath as he hastily returned his attention to the food that was cooking, now at accelerated heat. He put the sausages, somewhat charred from their extended frying, on the plates. Kelly dished out the salad. Troy removed the baked potatoes from the oven, sliced them in half and placed them on the plates. Kelly's prayer was briefer than usual, less animated than her customary enthusiastic saying of grace; Troy realized that she must be preoccupied by the encounter with Caroline Rancotti. Who shouldn't have gone to the library anyway. The library was closed to the public right now and wouldn't open—

"Amen."

"Amen," he added belatedly.

Kelly spread butter and sour cream on her potato; Troy did the same, adding other toppings that Kelly had brought from the refrigerator. It ought to have been an ordinary domestic scene, the sort that he and Kelly shared every evening at the end of the day, when coming home from work made every meal a private celebration of their lives together.

"Coffee?" Kelly asked, getting up from her chair.

"I forgot to make it," he said, rising.

"I can do it."

"No, I'll do it," he said. "I wanted to give you a break."

"It'll just take a minute," she said.

Her slim form made graceful work of the coffee making and he watched her with pleasure as she moved, scooping the ground coffee into the filter, filling the carafe with water, switching the button on, her physical activity as much of a ballet as he would ever want to watch.

She sat down while the coffee was brewing.

"I'm sorry," he said.

"What for?"

"The coffee . . ." Troy opened his hands in a defeated gesture. "I wanted everything to be ready for when you came home."

"It's just the coffee, Troy," she said, dismissing the matter as she returned to her seat. "The meal was all yours."

He wondered if she could feel it, the knife's edge of tension cutting the cozy domestic tableau into invisible shreds, even though nothing was overtly wrong and nothing had been said. She had to feel it.

"What did Caroline say?"

It was hard to remember the exact words, but the accusation remained clear in Kelly's thoughts. "She thinks that we—I—the library—will be glad to see her blamed, her and Keith, for the murder because we don't want to see a local person arrested."

"That's stupid. She's a local person."

"She's a newcomer," Kelly said.

"If it comes to that, I'm a newcomer too," he argued. "I asked her questions, I didn't accuse her."

"She seemed to feel like she's being singled out. She and Keith both."

"She's not. I didn't treat her any differently than I did any of the other people on the list who have keys. Oh, by the way, I have a feeling that Rich Barry—you know, your no-show board member?—I think he and his girlfriend are having trouble."

Kelly looked surprised. "How do you know?"

"While I was questioning him, she came into the house, walked up the stairs, never said a word. He watched her but didn't say anything. He looked like there was plenty to say."

"Does that make him a suspect?"

The question jarred him. What was Kelly's meaning? "I don't know," Troy said in irritation. "Everyone is a suspect right now until we know who was in the library that night. Footprints would have been covered over by the snow. It could have been anyone."

"Anyone with a key."

"Of course anyone with a key. The locks weren't forced. If someone came in the back, nobody would have noticed in that snow."

"You didn't tell me that the forensics teams confirmed that whoever came in used the back entrance," she said.

"It was obvious," Troy replied. "I didn't tell you because that's what we all assumed. We just needed to have it proven by the evidence."

"Is there anything else that you can tell me?"

"Look, Kelly, this is my job. I'm sorry that it's taken a different direction from when you and I were working together against the Starks, I'm sorry—"

"There's no need to be sorry, Troy. You're right. You're doing your job."

Kelly wasn't avoiding his gaze now. Her dark brown eyes were pinioning him with what seemed like an accusatory stare. "You're doing your job," she continued. "And I'm doing mine, or I will be as soon as we can open again. But now our jobs have intersected. They've done that in the past, I know that, and if I seem petulant now, I'm sorry. I know that you have to question people like Caroline Rancotti. But she's very angry and she said she won't be doing any more fundraisers for the library."

"Okay, well, that's unfortunate, but if that's the way she wants to be, there's nothing anyone can do about it. I think she's being childish."

"She feels like she's being accused of a terrible crime with no evidence. And in the meantime, she's angry at the library staff. We're a nonprofit, we have to be on good terms with local businesses. We need their support."

"What do you want me to do, Kelly? Excuse any potential suspects if they can claim absolution because they donate to the library?"

"That's not what I'm saying."

"It sure sounds like what you're meaning. It sounds like you're blaming me for interrogating the Rancottis because it might influence them into not supporting the library."

"That's not what I mean! That's not what I said!" Kelly exclaimed, angered that Troy could so completely have missed the point she was trying to make.

"Then what are you saying? Explain it to me. I'll try to understand," he said.

The food on their plates was getting cold, but neither one noticed, so embroiled were they in the discussion—neither wanted to concede that it was an argument—that touched on matters of significance to both of them. For Troy, being a police officer meant upholding the law and that meant that no one got special treatment. To Kelly, innocent meant to be treated not as a guilty person, but as one who was not accused of a crime. The world of law enforcement was perhaps more nuanced than either of them wanted to acknowledge. Kelly was hurt that Troy interpreted her concern for the Rancottis as a threat to the financial support they could provide for the library, and Troy was aggravated that his wife would expect him to treat suspects according to their personal causes.

"I don't want to fight about this," Kelly said wearily.

"Neither do I. That's not what I intended."

He picked up his fork. The sausages and the baked potato had gone cold. So much for his attempt to give Kelly a break by making supper. He decided that it was probably a good thing that he hadn't told Kelly that during the questioning, he'd noticed that

Caroline Rancotti didn't wear a wedding ring. When he commented on it, she said that she'd gained weight with her second child and had to have the ring cut off. She hadn't been happy at the question. Her husband had backed up her story. He wore his wedding ring.

20

SLEUTHING, LIBRARY STYLE

They kissed in the morning before leaving for work, but each was aware that there was a rift between them. Neither Troy nor Kelly wanted the rift to remain, but neither knew how to heal it.

When Kelly arrived at the library, Carmela was already processing the books that had been returned overnight.

"You look like you didn't sleep," Carmela observed.

Kelly took off her coat and hat and sat down to pull off her boots. The heavy snow had stopped, but each day brought a fresh inch or two. Temperatures had remained cold, leaving the remains of ice and snow from Winter Storm Sergei as mementoes of the season's power. She walked to work rather than driving; parking spaces were cleared rectangles between walls of piled snow that had frozen and wouldn't thaw until the temperatures rose. No one was using them for the library now, but Kelly had decided that she'd rather get the exercise, since running along the Trail wasn't possible now.

"I keep thinking about Caroline and what she said."

"She's wrong," Carmela said bluntly. "I wasn't Lyola Knesbit's killer, but I got questioned. I didn't raise a ruckus about it."

As Kelly recalled, Carmela had been extremely upset at the implication that she had been involved in the murder of Mrs. Knesbit. But that initial response had been overridden when Mrs. Stark ordered Carmela placed on leave from her job while the case proceeded. Later, Carmela's tires had been slashed by one of the malicious pranksters who worked for the Starks. She'd had a lot more to deal with than the Rancottis. Still . . .

"I think we have to try harder to figure out who killed that man," she said.

"How are we going to figure it out when the police don't even know the identity of the man who was killed?"

"Susan Callahan asked me for the list of the people who attended the wine and cheese party that the Rancottis gave. We still have that list, don't we?"

"It's just names on a sheet of tablet paper," Carmela said. "I can type it up so that it's readable."

"Thanks, that might get us started, and Trooper Callahan will be glad to get it. I meant to get to that sooner, I just got distracted, I guess. Where's Chloe? She's supposed to be in today."

"Oh, she called off. She and her loverboy are back together. He called her and apologized for being a jerk. So they're spending the day together. Going skiing."

"I guess it doesn't matter. She can come in another day. We're not open yet anyway."

"Caroline Rancotti called to say she wants to cancel her library membership. I don't know if she means she wants us to take her off the active patron list. I can mark it in the membership database so we don't send her anything until she cools off. Rich Barry called to resign from the board; small loss, since he's never at the meetings anyway. Lucas called, wanting to know when gaming days are going to start up again. Greg Sloan called; he's planning to move to Tennessee to be with Jessie; I guess she's having some problems with her pregnancy. He said we should find another cleaner; he's going to start a business down there. He's closed up his house. He's sorry to give us such short notice but he figured we'd understand."

"Of course . . . did you talk to any of these people or did they just leave messages?" They'd have to find a new cleaning service, but fortunately, since she and the staff had done their own scrubbing and the library hadn't been open to patrons, that wouldn't be a pressing matter for the coming week.

"Voicemail messages. There was one from Sarah Duso, too; she said that we can open Monday. She'll put an announcement in the newspapers and post it on social media. You know, I'm getting a little tired of Sarah Duso acting as if we're not to be trusted to take care of these things. Who does she think used to do them?"

Kelly agreed with Carmela but knew she couldn't choose sides in what could turn into a something complicated. "Maybe she thinks she's helping."

"She's not," Carmela said, stacking the books on the cart to be shelved. "She's picking up where Lois Stark left off. Why is she so determined to be the only one talking to the press? Why do we have to go through her? Maybe Troy should be questioning her a little more forcefully."

"I'd better call Sarah and let her know there's a vacancy on the board, with Rich resigning." Kelly thought back to Troy's comment about Rich's possible romantic problems. "I don't know much about Rich," she said, delicately trying to probe Carmela, who knew everyone and the gossip that went along with the knowledge, without setting off her co-worker's notoriously sensitive curiosity.

"He's been living with Olivia Kruger for the past year," Carmela said. "I heard they fight all the time."

"He works for the post office, right?"

"He used to," Carmela said. "He lost his job."

"With the post office?"

Carmela nodded. "I've never known anyone to lose a job with the post office," she said grimly. She sat down at the computer, but Kelly was barely aware of the staccato clicking of the keys as Carmela typed. Thinking about the murder and the killer and the various question marks hovering over the people she knew only in their library context consumed her mind.

Clearly, Rich Barry's loss of a job was a mark against him. In Settler Springs, employment was an indication of a person's stability. Losing his post office job immediately made him a puzzle piece. Now, if Troy's instincts were right, he might be about to lose his girlfriend as well. If there were signs of disruption in his life, could murder be the cause?

He had a library key.

What if he had taken the books on infidelity from the library? True, the topic was marital infidelity, but if a couple was having problems in their relationship, infidelity remained an almost insurmountable obstacle.

"Here's the list," Carmela said, handing a sheet of paper to Kelly.

"What—oh, the wine and cheese party list."

"You said you wanted it," Carmela reminded her.

"I do, I just was thinking about Rich Barry and who we'll get to replace him."

"Let Sarah figure it out. I'm sure she'll have someone in mind."

"I'm sure she will."

Kelly called Sarah to give her the news about Rich's resignation. Sarah was matter-of-fact. "Please call him and let him know that we need his resignation in writing. I'll speak to the Nominating Committee about finding a candidate to replace him. Do you have any thoughts on someone who might benefit the library?"

"Before all of this, I'd have said Caroline Rancotti."

"Not now," Sarah answered. "She might be a murderer."

"I don't think she did it, but I agree. This wouldn't be a good time to ask her. She's not very happy with the library right now."

"Why?"

"She feels that she's being targeted as a suspect because she's new in town."

"That's ludicrous. She's either a murderer or she isn't. If you think of anyone who should be considered, let me know."

Kelly promised to do so. At least, she thought as she went back to her office, Sarah was willing to have input from the staff on a replacement for Rich Barry.

Carmela was upstairs, shelving the children's books. Kelly reached for the telephone.

"Rich, hi, it's Kelly at the library. I'm sorry to learn that you're resigning from the board."

"Yeah, well, it's not really my kind of thing, y'know? And now with me being out of work, and with everything else that's going on—"

"Everything else?" she asked, hoping that her tone sounded merely concerned and not overly curious.

"Yeah, well . . . the truth is that me and Livvie . . . the counselor says we need to work on our relationship."

"Oh, I'm sorry to hear that—that you and Livvie are —it's a hard time, I'm sure. Is there anything that we can do? Any books that we could order from interlibrary loan? There are a lot of books out there on relationships." And maybe, she thought, he'd already availed himself of books from the library.

"Yeah, well, I'm not really much of a reader. I don't know why I agreed to go on the board back when Mrs. Stark asked me. Not that she was any great model, either. What's all this about that body that you found in the library? Do they know who did it?"

"No . . . actually, they don't even know who the person is," Kelly said.

"They still haven't identified the guy? I guess he's not from around here, then. You know, I heard that the Rancottis might be involved."

"I don't believe that at all!"

"Yeah, well, you just never know."

Kelly was so irritated by his assertion that she forgot to ask him to submit a letter of resignation from the board. She was sending him an email when Carmela returned.

"Those pranks must have been tied to the murder," she said. "Nothing has happened since."

"I don't know if anyone would try to come into the library now," Kelly said. "Not with an unsolved murder investigation still going on."

"Maybe. Did you notice anything on that list?"

"I haven't looked yet."

Carmela sighed heavily. "I don't know why you asked me to print it if you didn't need it."

"I do need it. I just haven't had a chance to look at it. I called Sarah to let her know about Rich, and then I called Rich."

"Oh," Carmela said, mollified. "I hope Sarah picks someone who'll come to the meetings."

"I would have suggested Caroline Rancotti before all of this happened."

Carmela was shaking her head. "Too dramatic," she said. "We don't need any more drama around here."

Kelly gave the list her full attention, but didn't spot a name of anyone who inspired a sense of suspicion. Most of the attendees had been library board members, volunteers, and regulars, all familiar names; even Tia Krymanski had shown up for the event. There was a handful of new names, people who had no connection to the library but were interested in the product of a new winery: John and Claudia Treveck; W.J. Michaels; Annette Stiller; Martin and Elke Guardino. Kelly decided that these people were surely off the list of suspects because they wouldn't have keys and wouldn't have known enough about the library layout or its inner workings.

"I guess that wasn't much of an idea," she admitted to Carmela as they sat down to their lunches. "The same people who are familiar with the library are the ones that the police already know about."

"We've got some patrons who get on the wrong side of me," Carmela admitted, "but none of them that seem like they'd murder anyone. I don't—oh, what does that old fool want? Can't he see we're closed?"

But Kelly was already walking toward the front door, having spied Mr. Porter as he knocked.

"Hello, Mr. Porter," she greeted him. "I'm afraid we aren't open yet. We plan to open next week, maybe as early as Monday."

"I'll be very glad of that," he said in his courteous way. "I've missed my daily visit and your charming company. But I didn't come to intrude. I found this in the back lot. I'm afraid I parked back there and shouldn't have; I got stuck in the snow. After trying to free up my wheels, I got out of the car and found that I'd dislodged this from the packed down snow."

"What is it? It looks like a cell phone."

"I believe it is. Perhaps one of your clientele lost it and has been looking for it. Buried in as much snow as was there, it might not have appeared until spring. I hope I didn't damage it."

"It looks to be intact, although I don't know how well it'll work after being buried in the snow. But thank you, Mr. Porter, I'll check it and we'll see if we can return it to its owner."

Mr. Porter tipped his hat. "Please convey my regards to Miss Dixon," he said. "I look forward to seeing her as well next week after the library opens again. I've quite missed my daily visits."

"We've missed you too, Mr. Porter," Kelly said, lying about Carmela in the quest for politeness.

"What did he want?" Carmela asked when Kelly returned to the table.

"He had parked in the back lot, and got stuck. He was trying to get his car out of the snow when he got out and noticed that all the movement had dislodged this cell phone. Someone must have lost it."

"I don't know why the old fool parked back there," Carmela grumbled. "We're closed."

"He might have wanted to see if we were open," Kelly said. "Anyway, we'll try to find out whose phone this is."

"If it's been in the snow, it probably won't work."

"If it's been in the snow . . . it must have been lost the night of the storm," Kelly said, her thoughts racing. "What if—Carmela, what if it belongs to the killer?"

21

THE CELL PHONE

Troy wasn't optimistic that the cell phone would still work, but he was grateful for anything that could possibly provide a lead to the murder investigation. He was also relieved that, with the discovery of the phone, some of the strain that had developed between him and Kelly was easing.

"It might not be anything," he cautioned that evening as they went for supper at the Pizzaria, both of them tacitly eager to avoid a meal at home with the memory of the previous evening still fresh. "The phone might not be working. But Susan seemed happy that you found it."

"Mr. Porter found it, I didn't. He dropped it off today. But it must have been lost the night of the storm, right? And buried underneath the snow?"

"It seems likely," Troy, ever cautious, wasn't going to gallop into speculation until Susan had had a chance to have the phone checked out by people who knew what they were doing.

"You were right about Rich Barry," Kelly said.

"Who? Oh, the board member."

"He resigned from the board. He and his girlfriend are having problems, just as you suspected. But I don't think he's the killer."

Troy, a generous slice of pizza liberally dotted with pepperoni halfway to his lips, paused before biting into it. "What gave you the idea that he's a suspect?"

"You went back to question him."

"I went back to question everyone on the key list."

"Oh, well, he's not a reader. I don't think he took those books out."

"What books?"

"The books on marital infidelity," she answered. "The ones that Carmela found in the book drop," she explained. "When she shelved them and found the wine glasses."

"Oh . . . I'd forgotten about the wine glasses," he said. "Except in connection with the Rancottis." Troy frowned.

"What's the matter?"

He decided not to tell Kelly that Susan Callahan intended to bring Caroline down to the station for fingerprinting, and to try on the wedding ring. The ring had been wiped clean of any evidence, so it was unlikely that they'd learn anything unless Caroline's prints were already in the database, and even that wouldn't tell them much unless she had a previous murder charge, which wasn't likely. Even if the ring fit, Susan admitted, it wouldn't reveal much. Ring sizes weren't unique.

"Nothing," he said. "I'm just trying to figure out how the library ties in with all of this."

"So am I," Kelly nodded. "I went back over the list of the people who attended the wine and cheese party, but I couldn't see a connection. There are people who have nothing to do with the library, and they don't have keys. There are people who are connected to the library and have keys, but you've already talked to them. There are library regulars and volunteers who attended; they know the library, they know how to find a book, but they don't have keys and they couldn't get in on their own. I'm sorry about the way I acted last night."

It was a non sequitur, but Troy practically leaped upon it. "Me, too," he said eagerly. "I didn't mean to get on your last nerve."

"You didn't. I should be able to separate what you're doing from what I'm doing. I'm so used to thinking of everything in terms of how it affects the library that I wasn't fair to you."

"Don't be too contrite," he warned with a grin. "You don't know what I'll demand by way of an apology."

She grinned back. "I already apologized. And so did you. So we're even."

Troy sighed in contentment. "I'll be glad when the snow melts and we can run on the Trail again," he said.

Kelly nodded. "Back to normal. I never realized how comforting a routine is until now. The library closed because of this, the Trail so snow covered that we can't use it . . . it feels like somebody came in with a machete and chopped out a huge piece of our normal lives." She sobered. "I guess I shouldn't gripe, though. That man who was murdered. Even though we don't know who he is, there must be someone who would miss him. Someone must care if he's alive or not."

"Someone cared enough to want him dead and gone," Troy reminded her.

"I know, I haven't forgotten that. But why bring him to the library? That's what still makes no sense. If you were going to kill someone, wouldn't you try to hide the body so that no one would know what you did?"

"In the first place," Troy said, extending his hand across the table to touch hers, "I'm not planning to kill anyone."

"I know that, but if you did, it would be a crime of passion in the first place. You'd do it impulsively, suddenly. You wouldn't give the person a sleeping pill, then stab him, then put his jacket back on and take him to the library and leave him in the romance section."

"No," Troy conceded. "I wouldn't do that. Whoever did this was making a point. We just don't know who he was making it to."

"You said 'he,'" Kelly pounced. "Caroline Rancotti couldn't have lifted that man and lugged him into the library."

"No. But Keith could have. Keith is a big guy, keeps fit. He's active; he doesn't sit around all day, sipping wine. He's lifting boxes, he's unloading deliveries . . . he could have helped."

"Troy, do you really think they're guilty?"

Troy thought before he spoke, not wanting to ignite another disagreement on the subject of the Rancottis that would inspire Kelly to rush to their defense. He knew how loyal she was and most of the time, he valued that quality. But there were times when loyalty could be misplaced or abused and it was possible that this was one of those times.

"I don't know who did this, Kelly," he said, keeping his hand on hers as a connection in case his words served to separate them. "Whoever did it has to be punished for it. That's the law. I hope it's not them, I can say that much. We don't know anything. Maybe the cell phone will give up its secrets. Maybe it won't."

But several days later, when Susan Callahan came into the police station, entered his office and closed the door behind her, she had a look on her face that spoke volumes.

"Wyatt James Michaels," she said with an exuberance that was foreign to her.

"Wyatt—Michaels . . . W.J. Michaels?" he asked, recalling the name on the list of people who had attended the library's wine and cheese fundraiser in early December.

"It's his cell phone. He might be our victim. I've sent out bulletins with his name and photograph. I think we'll be able to get his identity confirmed by the weekend. And Caroline Rancotti's cell phone number is one of his contacts."

"Do we bring her in? The wedding ring idea didn't pan out; it didn't fit her," Troy reminded, remembering how irate Caroline Rancotti had been when she was fingerprinted, and how triumphant she'd been when she tried on the ring, as Troy directed, but it was too big for her finger. She had made vague threats about suing the police department for harassment; Keith, her husband, had urged her to be quiet but Caroline had unleashed a stream of invective against the police department, the library, and Settler Springs that could not be stemmed. Then she'd stormed out of the police station. Her husband had paused to apologize for her behavior, but then he'd just said, "You don't understand," and he'd followed her out the door. Being in the alleged victim's list of phone contacts was damning, but Troy didn't want to proceed with an arrest until they were sure that Caroline Rancotti was guilty of murder.

Susan shook her head. "Not yet. I'm investigating the Rancottis from when they lived in Pittsburgh. Did they live near this guy? Was there a personal or professional connection? Did they really leave because they wanted to raise their kids in a small town or was that just an excuse for something else. When we get her, we need to have everything lined up in a row. Every last duck, right down to the quack and waddle."

"Yeah," Troy agreed.

"You sound disappointed."

"No," Troy corrected her. "It's never pleasant when a murderer is someone you know, even if it's not a close acquaintance. I know her through the library, through Kelly."

"Kelly will be troubled at this."

"Kelly is troubled by murder," he corrected her again, determined to made the single-minded state trooper realize that there were many layers to his wife and they all included compassion.

"It's her assistance that could break this. She told us about the wine and cheese fundraiser, she provided the list of people who attended, she gave us the cell phone. Will she be able to handle the fact that her assistance is what could break this case for us?"

"Kelly won't hide a murderer," Troy said patiently. "Murder is a sin. Don't mistake Kelly's compassion for her commandments. She knows right from wrong."

"I hope you're right," Susan Callahan said, her features once more composed into their deadpan expression. "Because if the accusation has merit and the case goes to trial, Kelly will be called to testify against Caroline Rancotti."

22

"IT'S SOMEONE WE KNOW"

Kelly had been hesitant about how to reopen the library. Too much celebration ignored the fact that a deadly, premeditated crime had been committed before the body was brought to the library for discovery. Too little, and they would seem oblivious to the community's appreciation of the library as an institution.

Carmela, for whom gardening was a passion, brought in half a dozen plants from home and placed them throughout the library, upstairs and downstairs. "Plants make a place look alive," she said gruffly, as if fearful that she had been caught in a frivolous act. "We want people to think of something besides death here."

In the end, they decided to continue with the library's usual procedures. March was Women's History Month, so there was a display celebrating the role that females had played in history. The first day of spring would be arriving soon, which led Chloe to decorate the Children's Corner with lions and lambs and pictures of flowers. St. Patrick's Day was approaching, a reason to adorn the library with cut-out, construction paper shamrocks. March was a versatile month with an ample palette of images from which to choose.

The staff arrived early that Monday and surveyed their efforts before opening the doors. Already, there were people outside. While some were there, Kelly knew, because they missed being able to come to the library, others were there out of morbid curiosity.

"It looks very nice," Sarah Duso said. "You've all done a wonderful job. And I love the plants; I hope you'll keep them." She was there in her role as library board president, but also to be the spokesperson for the library should anyone have questions regarding the murder. Carmela was irritated by the decision but Kelly was resigned to it. Troy had said that it was better for her if Sarah was the one to address the questions. 'Let her be associated with it,' he'd suggested. 'You and Carmela and Chloe can go on being what you already are. You're the ones the community looks to. When this all fades, you'll still be the ones they look to.'

It made sense and Kelly had decided that Troy was right. That was why she had decided not to bake cookies or have coffee for patrons to enjoy on this reopening day. Until the killer was caught and the murder solved, the library could not forget what had happened.

The patrons came in, looking around curiously as if they expected something to be different. The media had not mentioned where the body had been discovered, so they were spared the images of people prowling the romance section for its role as a crime scene.

Doug Iolus, cameras as always around his neck, strolled in with the others and headed straight for Sarah after giving Kelly a raised-eyebrow glance that told her he somehow knew the protocol. He asked for an interview and Sarah agreed. Patrons went in search of books, most of them anyway. Several came straight to the desk.

"How awful for you, Kelly, to have found the body," said Leah Delano, a library regular who usually had her three children in tow with her when she made the weekly visit to the library.

"I'm glad we're open again," Kelly said evenly. "You don't have the kids today?"

"No, well, I just didn't think it was right, you know, with everything that happened."

"Chloe will be disappointed. She's spent a lot of time on the March decorating and displays. Some new books came in; you might want to look at them before someone else checks them out."

Leah was nosy, but she was a fervent believer in reading to her children. She thanked Kelly and headed for the stairs to the Children's Corner.

"Well done, you deflected that nicely," Doug, having made an arrangement to talk with Sarah that afternoon, came up to the desk. He turned his back to Kelly, aimed his camera, and took photos of the people filling the building. Then he turned around again. "Rough time."

She knew that even though Doug was a journalist, he was a friend. "I'll be glad when it's over," she said. "When they've caught the murderer and the case is closed and we can all go on—" she paused. "I guess we can't go on as before," she acknowledged.

"You'll go on," Doug replied. "But someone is the murderer and it's someone we know."

She looked at him, startled by his assessment. He was correct, she knew he was but somehow, she hadn't considered the matter so starkly.

"You look surprised," he said. "Someone got into the library. That's not a stranger, as much as we'd like it to be."

Kelly looked around the library. Sarah Duso was talking to another member of the media, a reporter for a Pittsburgh newspaper. Scavengers, she thought, coming to the library to pick up carrion from a dead body that might as well still be here, the way that everyone was acting.

"I suppose," she said. Someone came to the desk to check out books then, and she was relieved to be able to resume her normal role. She wondered where Carmela was and then spied her, over by the magazines, next to Mr. Porter. They appeared to be in conversation.

Kelly smiled. Maybe, maybe, something good would come out of all of this, if at the very least, Carmela could come to see Mr. Porter in a less hostile light.

There weren't any children present, but that probably wasn't a surprise, although Chloe was likely to be disappointed. Monday wasn't her usual working day but she wanted to be present for the reopening. She was aglow now that she and her fiancé had made up and were once again together. In the meantime, Leah Delano would get Chloe's full attention with suggestions for books for her children. Parents with preschoolers would want to avoid the library in its initial reopening, rather than have their children picking up bits of conversation that would require unpleasant discussions. After school, kids would come in again, the older ones on their own, the younger ones with parents, and by then, the volume of people would be less, as the curious returned home, their inquisitiveness eased if not sated.

"I think it's going well," Sarah said after Kelly had checked out books for another patron, one who was distinctly irritated by people coming into the library just to "rubberneck" as she put it. She said she'd be back tomorrow when she wouldn't have to push her way through people to get her books. But she wasn't annoyed at the library or Kelly.

"I hope so."

"Don't you think so?"

"Once the talk dies down and the case is solved, maybe everything will be okay."

"Oh, but that won't be for a while, you know," Sarah said. "They still have to identify the victim, then find the killer, and there will be months before the trial. I'm afraid that we'll have to adapt to the fact that the library is going to be in the news for some time."

Noticing Kelly's downcast expression, Sarah said, "But you organized the reopening perfectly. It's not a wake for the dead man and it's not a celebration either. It's the library and that's what we need. Things won't be back to normal for a while, but it starts today, and I think that's what we need. I was afraid that we'd have to postpone our annual solicitation campaign if the library was still a place of notoriety, but I think we can continue as usual."

She and Kelly made arrangements to meet later in the week to outline the campaign and to decide what they would highlight as the library's achievements and needs in order to elicit financial support from donors.

"We can't send a letter to the Rancottis," Kelly told her. "She asked to be taken off the mailing list and to cancel her membership."

"Oh, really," Sarah said scornfully. "She's overreacting. The police are talking to everyone. They interrogated me because I have a key, but I'm not throwing a tantrum over it. I had no idea she was so volatile."

"I can't blame her for being upset, though," Kelly said. "She's a businesswoman and the winery is just getting off the ground. She doesn't want the adverse publicity to hurt the winery's prospects."

"Kelly, you see the good in everyone. That's commendable. Maybe in time, she'll come around and realize that the library is not at fault here. But in the meantime, we'll approach the usual businesses for support—"

Doug Iolus was coming their way. "I'm on my way to the state police station," he said. "Thought you should know. They've called Caroline Rancotti in for questioning for the murder of Wyatt Michaels. They've identified the victim. I just got the text."

"Who texted you?" Kelly asked.

"Not Troy," Doug grinned briefly. "Gotta go. I got a tip. The victim was at the wine and cheese party."

Kelly and Sarah looked at each other in dismay. If the victim had been identified as someone who had attended the wine and cheese fundraiser, and Caroline Rancotti was the killer, the library would not avoid the spotlight any time soon.

23

SECRETS

"**T**ell them, Caroline."

This was from Keith Rancotti, standing by his wife's side in the police station. "She didn't kill Wyatt, officer," Keith said earnestly.

"She lied about knowing him." There was no change of tone in Susan Callahan's voice, but there was no mistaking the seriousness of her manner.

Caroline was sobbing. "Yes, I knew him! I—knew him."

"How well did you know him?"

Caroline's sobbing prevented her from answering. Keith answered. "Caroline met Wyatt Michaels last year; he said he was a freelance journalist who worked for outlets that covered wines."

"That was true!" Caroline burst out. "I checked; his stories were in some of the more prominent magazines. He wrote well . . . I thought that we would benefit from the coverage. Our winery was doing well, and we were planning to expand and come here, just like I said. We want the girls to grow up knowing their neighbors . . . that's what we did want then."

"When did you meet him?"

"It was in the summer. Keith and I were busy with the Pittsburgh winery and then the renovation of the church here in Settler Springs to start up the second winery. We knew it was going to be a challenge to keep both wineries going but we thought we could do it. Then Wyatt suggested that he would like to be taken on as a—a kind of trainee. He wanted to write his story from the perspective of someone juggling a new winery and an established one. It seemed like a good idea, and a different angle, and we . . . I said okay. It meant spending a lot of time with Wyatt. Keith was busy. I was busy, too. Wyatt was . . . there," she added on a forlorn note that revealed much about how she had become involved with him. "But I didn't kill him!"

"I found out what was going on," Keith continued. "I told Caroline that she had to choose. And she did. She agreed to break it off with Michaels."

"According to the telephone records, his last call to you was in December. Do you remember that call?"

"I blocked his number," Caroline said.

"When did you break off the affair?"

"In October."

"But he called you in December."

"He didn't call until then. I don't know what he wanted. I blocked his number when I saw it on my phone," Caroline said. "I recognized it, I didn't want to talk to him. When I saw him at the library for the wine and cheese fundraiser, I didn't know why he was there."

"It must have created a certain amount of tension."

"I avoided him. Keith and I both avoided him. And he didn't approach us. He was writing a story."

"Did he ever submit the story?"

"I haven't seen it," Caroline said. "But I didn't ask him. I didn't talk to him. He walked around the library, sampling the wines, but he didn't interview people or tell people who he was. I know that because someone would have commented on it to me. He was there for an hour or so and then he left. Keith and I were so upset, but I never heard from him again. I didn't want to!"

"It's strange that you didn't block his number right away, after you broke off the affair," Susan commented.

"He said he wouldn't contact me. I believed him. And he didn't. We came here, and we got involved in the community. It's what we wanted. Small-town life. We offered to do the wine and cheese fundraiser and the library staff was appreciative. It was a success!" Caroline said defiantly, looking to Troy for confirmation. "Kelly must have told you that."

"She did," Troy said. "She was very grateful."

"I didn't kill him! I had no reason to even think of doing something like that. He wasn't a threat to me."

"Then why did he show up at the fundraiser? How did he find out about it?"

"We publicized it extensively," Keith answered. "We wanted to reach out beyond the local community. We had people in Pittsburgh who were interested in what we were doing. We wanted the library to have a good turnout."

"So Mr. Michaels was still following your career."

"I don't know. He wrote about wine. I suppose he was connected with every winery in the local area. But he wrote on a national level, too. He traveled a lot. He had an unpredictable schedule; he would suddenly just show up after being away for a few days. I didn't think about it. He was just suddenly there again. He was—"

"What was he like?"

Keith answered. "When we first met him, he had a very sophisticated appearance. No beard, no faux rustic look. Cosmopolitan. Sophisticated. Very charming," he said, a note of bitterness in his intonation. "He traveled a lot, and he country-dropped. France, Greece, Italy . . . I thought of him as the bouquet."

"The bouquet?"

"In winemaking, it's the aromas. Wine acquires different smells as it ages. It's what the wine is doing while it's waiting to be ready," Keith tried to explain. "Michaels never worked in a vineyard, he didn't know how much effort goes into winemaking or into starting up a winery. He liked the image of wine drinking as much as he liked its taste."

Susan's gaze cut to Troy's and he knew that she was puzzled by Keith's answer.

"Was that a description of him as a womanizer as well?" Troy asked.

"I assume so. I don't think there was much substance to him, beyond the image. Look," Keith said impatiently, "Caroline and I are working on things. We're going to counseling. This thing, this, this infidelity, it cut me to the bone. I gave her a choice and I meant what I said: leave him or I leave. She chose me. We have two daughters. We share a business. We're married, we share dreams . . . we're trying to rebuild our marriage. I think we're succeeding. When I saw him at the library that night, I admit that my first reaction was that he had wanted to start things up again."

"You didn't think that your wife might have been the one who wanted to start things up again?" Susan asked.

Keith shook his head emphatically. "She knew what she had done. She knew it was wrong. She didn't want him ruining our marriage. He left the library and I never saw him again."

"I never did either. But when I saw the description and the photo, and I heard what happened, I couldn't tell you that I knew him. You'd think I killed him. And you'd think that Keith had helped me, because you'd know I couldn't have carried him into the library by myself. But that week, we were both planning for the First Responders Valentine's Day Dance. We weren't planning a murder! How could we possibly have been planning to kill Wyatt while we were working on the wines for the dance?"

"The dance was cancelled. By the beginning of the week, it was apparent that the storm was going to hit."

Caroline shook her head. "It was likely that the storm would hit," she corrected. "We didn't know. Jimmy cancelled it several days before the dance. Thursday! He cancelled it on Thursday. The newspapers said the body was found on Friday morning. We couldn't have shifted plans that fast. And we didn't!"

"Your daughters were with their grandparents. Even after the dance was cancelled, you didn't bring them home."

"They like being with their grandparents. We knew school would be cancelled on Friday. Keith and I

224

thought that we'd just enjoy the time together. We'd been so busy working that we hadn't had much leisure time. This seemed like it would make up for some of that."

Keith, still stalwart at his wife's side, spoke up. "You don't have any real evidence against Caroline," he said. "It's all circumstantial."

"We're still investigating," Susan Callahan told him calmly. "I'm sure we'll be in touch with you again."

"You'd better go now," Troy said. "I'm sure the press folks have already heard that you're here and they'll be gathering."

Keith nodded and helped Caroline to her feet. "We didn't do it," he said as they paused by the station door. "I guess you hear that all the time. But we didn't do it."

"It doesn't matter now," Caroline cried. Her makeup was ruined by the rivulets of tears that had streamed down her cheeks. "In the eyes of Settler Springs, we'll always be suspect. No one is going to patronize our winery, they'll associate us with a murder. Especially when this all comes out."

"Nothing is 'out', Mrs. Rancotti," Susan said. "What was said in this office hasn't been shared. We're still investigating. Expect to see us again."

When he and Susan Callahan were once again alone in the office, Troy said, "Do you think she's guilty?"

Susan made a face. "No. There's no evidence that ties them to the body. We've checked their home, we checked their Pittsburgh winery . . . nothing. If we pushed this now, we'd only ruin their reputations and the case would be thrown out. But if we don't find the killer soon, we won't be able to prevent judgment from falling on the Rancottis and ruining their lives. I want a conviction, I don't want character assassination."

24

THE WINE JOURNALIST

Kelly had been worried when Troy said to meet him for lunch at The Café. Doug's words had created an accelerating sense of anxiety within her and as the morning went on with no information, she found it almost impossible to think clearly. The throng of people eventually thinned out and the library returned to its morning routine.

Carmela was unusually quiet as she worked at the desk. Mr. Porter had left, but not before telling Kelly and Carmela how pleased he was to be able to come to the library again. This time, Carmela had not disputed his statement with scorn. Upstairs, Chloe worked on that week's story hour program. Sarah had left for her interview with Doug.

Kelly sat in her office, staring at the computer screen and ostensibly making up a book order for the latest releases coming out. Troy's phone call offered little explanation, but Kelly was glad to hear from him and she was already seated in their customary booth when he walked in.

"Doug said that Caroline Rancotti was at the state police station," she said as soon as he sat down.

Troy unbuttoned his winter jacket and took it off as small flakes of snow flew around him. "It's snowing again," he said, unnecessarily.

"Did she—is she arrested?"

Francie came over with coffee for both of them. "Kelly already ordered for you," she said as Troy asked for a menu. She grinned. "See the advantages of being married? You don't even have to think. She'll do it for you."

Troy smiled. "That's only one of the advantages of being married."

"Your order will be up in a few minutes," Francie promised.

When they were alone, Kelly repeated her question. "Doug got a tip telling him that Caroline was at the police station. Did you arrest her?"

"No."

Kelly didn't hide her relief. "Thank God," she said.

"What if she turns out to be the murderer?" he inquired.

"She's not."

"You know that? You're that sure?"

"I just don't believe she killed that guy. Or anyone. Doug said he's been identified and he was at the wine and cheese event? I was there, why didn't I recognize him?"

Troy recalled what Keith said. "Apparently, he'd grown a beard since December, and he was cultivating a rugged look. A completely different appearance, from what they recalled."

"Nobody else recognized him either. The library regulars, they must have seen him."

"Probably. But they didn't know who he was. It was before Christmas. People see a lot of people. I'm not surprised that no one recognized the photograph. There was the difference in appearance and the difference between life and death."

"How is Caroline?"

"Upset. She knew him from the winery they have in Pittsburgh," Troy said, carefully calculating how much he could tell Kelly and how much had to remain confidential. There was no reason to share the news of Caroline's infidelity; Susan Callahan had promised that information would not be shared. If subsequent events pointed a more damning finger at the Rancottis, that would change. "He's a journalist who covers wines."

"A journalist. Really? That's . . ." Kelly frowned.

"What's the matter?"

"Someone was asking me about articles that a journalist had written for the wine magazine niche. Who was it? . . . I can't remember. It was awhile ago."

"Before the murder?"

"I don't know. Why?" she asked, alerted by his attention that his question wasn't without a purpose. "Does it matter?"

"I don't know." *Would Caroline have researched articles by her former lover before the murder?* By then, she already had vetted his journalistic credentials and knew that he was what he claimed to be. She'd already become intimately involved with him, been discovered in her affair by her husband, and broken it off. Besides, Caroline didn't seem as though she'd need to ask a librarian to find a magazine article for her. He knew that the Rancottis had a website; he'd checked it out as part of the investigation. So who else might have been curious?

"Do you get a lot of questions like that?"

"You mean questions about articles written in wine magazines?" Kelly asked, amused. "None. We always get offbeat questions, but they're always different. Who asked me that? . . ."

Their meals arrived; a burger and fries for Troy, salad for Kelly. After Francie left, Troy again pressed Kelly.

"Is there any record?"

"Of a question? No, we don't record reference questions. Besides, she just—it was a woman who asked. Someone . . . I remember that I was surprised by the question because it didn't come from someone who would have been all that interested in wine."

"Were you able to answer the question?"

"I found the articles she was looking for. By a Wyatt Michaels—why did he give his initials when he reserved a spot for the wine and cheese party?" Kelly asked.

"Maybe he didn't want Caroline to know he was coming. You saw a W.J. Michaels and didn't think anything of it."

"I didn't think anything of Wyatt Michaels, either," Kelly retorted. "I'd never heard of him. We do get a wine magazine, the Rancottis sponsor it, and people do read it. Mr. Porter reads it."

"Mr. Porter? Carmela's would-be sweetheart?"

"He reads a lot of things. He has a lot of interests. Actually, he and Carmela were talking today. Really. In the magazine section. And she didn't have anything cutting to say after he left. It was when everyone came in this morning, when we opened."

"How was it?" Troy asked. He wanted to press Kelly to remember who had asked for information on the journalist, now identified as Wyatt Michaels, but memory wasn't so easily lassoed. Better to let her recall it gradually, so that she'd remember more of the setting and the person asking the question.

"I felt like we were a circus act. Some people were normal, like always, they wanted books and they didn't come to ogle a murder scene. Others were obviously there for information. Doug was there, but it's his job. Other reporters were there. City reporters."

"It's their job, too," he reminded her, still sensitive on the topic of what a person had to do because a job required it, even if it wasn't something pleasant or congenial.

"I know," she sighed. "They were orderly. Sarah talked to them. You were right about not minding if she wants to be the face of the library for this investigation. I didn't have to bother about what to say or what not to say. I could turn the subject back to books."

"I'm glad it wasn't too bad."

"How was it at the station? Doug left because he got a tip. I imagine other reporters got tips too."

"Doug has sources everywhere. City reporters wouldn't have the same sources. I was afraid it would be a circus. We told the Rancottis to leave and not to linger, but I didn't see a swarm out there. I suppose Doug was there, but the Rancottis left the parking lot without anyone following them."

"Good. They've had enough to deal with."

It wasn't over yet, Troy thought as he and Kelly continued eating and chatting about other things, the subject of the murder investigation tabled, at least for the time being. Susan Callahan didn't want to arrest anyone until she had an airtight case, but Troy knew that if more evidence came along that conclusively tied Caroline and Keith to the murder, Susan would move quickly. As she should. As he would, if the arrest were his to make. Friends or not, library supporters or not, murder wasn't something that could be excused by bonds of loyalty.

He returned to the police station with a feeling of optimism. Kelly had a phenomenal memory. It wasn't always straightforward and tiered in logical progression, but that wasn't the kind of memory that made her the fantastic librarian she was. She could make connections that weren't always linear. He knew the wheels would be turning inside her thoughts, even as she went about her business.

In the meantime, all he could do was wait. There was no sense in bringing this up to Susan Callahan, who was entirely linear in her approach to crime solving. Because the ring found in the shelving section where Michaels' body had been found did not fit Caroline, the state trooper was inclined to dismiss it as a piece of evidence. She had the same lack of interest in the engagement ring found in the Children's Corner. The wine glasses that showed up where the books on marital infidelity were shelved were likewise discounted as insignificant.

But Troy couldn't help but think that there was something, or someone, as yet unrevealed. Once that missing puzzle piece was found, they'd have the reason why the journalist was killed. And they'd know who did it.

25

MAKING THE CONNECTION

"**J**essie Sloan!"

Kelly sat up in bed. Beside her, Troy groaned and immediately glanced at the clock by his side of the bed. Three o'clock in the morning. Well before either he or Kelly had to get up. "What's wrong?" he asked groggily.

"Jessie Sloan. She was the one who wanted to know about the man who'd written the articles on wine. Jessie Sloan. She didn't usually come into the library, we almost never saw them. But this time she came in and she asked a library question. She wanted to read the articles by a journalist named Wyatt Michaels. I'd never heard of him, but I looked him up on the Internet for her and I found his Linked-In page. Jessie wasn't comfortable with computers; she and

Greg don't own one. I'm surprised they have a cell phone. I guess they needed it for their clients. I found the article in the magazine that we had and I said I could get others from a magazine database. She said that was okay, she'd just read the article from the magazine that we subscribe to. I got it for her, she read it and that was the end of it. I never gave it a second thought, except to think it was unusual. But that was after you'd been shot and I wasn't very focused on anything but you."

"I thought you said she left to go to Tennessee or somewhere to have her baby."

"That's what Caroline told me. In February. Jessie and Greg have suffered through so many miscarriages. Greg would leave notes for us when Jessie couldn't come to clean with him and he was rearranging his schedule. He didn't go into a lot of detail, he just wrote that she'd been disappointed again. One time, he came in and I asked him if she was better. That's when I learned that "disappointed again" was a euphemism for a miscarriage. But she was finally pregnant again. I think they'd stopped trying and all of a sudden, she was expecting. She wanted to go home to Tennessee, to be near her mother while she was pregnant. Greg was okay with it. She had already gone down, and Greg was planning to visit her for Valentine's Day. The weekend of the storm. You remember. He was going to leave early so that he could beat the storm. We got a phone call from him last week. He decided to stay in Tennessee with Jessie. He's going to start a cleaning business there."

"He's not coming back here to settle things first?"

"I guess she's having problems with her pregnancy. Greg thought it would be better if he stayed there with her. I didn't talk to him; he left a message on the phone and Carmela told me. He said he'd closed up his house."

Troy sat up and turned on the lamp next to the bed. He was wide awake. "When did you get the call?"

"It was the day after you talked to Rich Barry," Kelly said.

The day after he and Kelly argued over the Rancottis.

"So he went down, decided to stay there, came back here to close up the house and didn't stop by in person to tell his clients that he wasn't going to be cleaning for them? Didn't stop in to let you or any of his clients know what he was going to do? He came back and then when he was back in Tennessee, he called you to let you know he wouldn't be returning?"

"I guess . . . yes. I didn't pay a lot of attention because we'd been cleaning and I figured we had time before we had to hire a new service. I should have paid more attention but—"

"Do you have his phone number? His cell phone number?"

"It's at the library. Oh, but I have it in my phone, too. Why? Troy, you don't think—"

"I don't know what I think, but something's out of place here. Maybe. Maybe I'm just grasping at straws," Troy said as he got out of bed and pulled on jeans and a sweatshirt. "I need that number and Susan needs to know this. We have to check his house."

"I want to come with you," Kelly said immediately, swinging her feet over the side of the bed.

"You can't, Kelly. I wish you could. But you can't. I have to present all this to Susan, and she has to make a judgment. I think she'll agree, and then we have to get authorization to go into the Sloans' house."

"A warrant?"

"A search warrant. Without a lot of evidence. It won't be easy. I promise you, I'll call you as soon as I know what we're going to do."

He could see that she was reluctant to accept his explanation, but he knew that his Kelly would realize why this investigation had to proceed in a legal, orderly matter. Someone had killed Wyatt Michaels and maybe, just maybe, the Sloans were involved. It was flimsy, but compared to the circumstantial evidence they had on the Rancottis, and the nothing that they had on anyone, it was a possibility.

Kelly walked down the stairs with him, Arlo following behind. She kissed him at the door.

"Be careful," she said automatically.

"If he's in Tennessee," Troy pointed out, "he'd have to be some shot to reach me here."

"Just be careful anyway."

She watched him get into the Suburban and pull out of the driveway. Sleep was not going to come now, so she went to the kitchen and boiled hot water for tea. Then she sat on the couch, her mind swerving between prayer and the unanswered questions about the murder as if her thoughts were driving out of control on a superspeed highway.

Why had Jessie Sloan wanted to read articles written for wine magazines by a journalist named Wyatt Michaels? Jessie and Greg lived out in the country, on the land that had belonged to his family for generations. They lived a rather rustic life, proud of taking care of themselves. They heated their home with a woodstove and they maintained a garden. They both hunted and lived off what they caught. They didn't have cable television. They made their own musical instruments and liked to play and sing together in the evenings, Kelly knew; Jessie had told her that on one of the rare occasions when she'd come into the library. They worked on weekends and evenings, when the buildings they cleaned were unoccupied. Jessie was the outgoing one, Greg kept to himself. But they had seemed suited for one another, at least that was the assumption Kelly had made, based on—based on what?

She'd filled in the blanks herself, she realized. Jessie's conversation was about her flowers, her garden, her dulcimer. Greg didn't talk much; when he did, it was about his work or about his wife. He seemed to cherish her.

They kept to themselves. Not in isolation; there were times when they were in the library. Jessie made her own deer jerky, and at Christmas time, she brought some in for the staff and board, along with homemade Christmas cookies. Greg worked with wood and always brought along something he'd carved for the library. The board gave them an annual bonus at Christmastime.

But Jessie hadn't come in this year for Christmas. Greg had left their presents on the circulation desk; he'd come in to pick up his check and he'd left the presents. Kelly had been so occupied with concern for Troy that she hadn't really paid attention to anything else. Carmela had told her that Greg Sloan had dropped off the Christmas presents and Carmela had put Kelly's gifts on her desk.

When, then, had Jessie asked about the magazine articles? And why? She hadn't seen Jessie at all this year, and hadn't seen her at Christmas last year. But Jessie had definitely come into the library when Kelly was there, to ask about the magazine writer.

Greg hadn't been with her. That was unusual; Jessie and Greg were always together. At least, she was always with him, never by herself.

Kelly tried to reconstruct the months backwards in her mind. Nothing tugged at her memory for December, except for the wine and cheese fundraiser. But Jessie hadn't attended the function. Why then, had she come in after that, but before Christmas, to ask for magazine articles by Wyatt Michaels? Had she met him somehow? But how would a woman who ran a cleaning business with her husband meet a magazine writer who specialized in wine? It didn't make sense.

Maybe this was all the wildest of goose chases, Kelly thought wearily. She put away her cup and went back upstairs to bed. She turned out the light, hoping that darkness would bring slumber. But her thoughts were too jumbled and too many questions swirled around in her mind. Jessie Sloan. Greg Sloan. Wyatt Michaels, or W.J. Michaels.

There was no point of connection. Wyatt Michaels had no connection with the library until the day his dead body was brought inside. Jessie Sloan had no connection to Wyatt Michaels until she asked about the magazine articles he'd written. But why had she asked?

She longed to call Troy and ask him if he'd learned anything yet, but she knew she couldn't. He was working on the investigation, sharing what he knew with Susan Callahan, and both of them would be engrossed in the case, even though it was still so early in the morning that dawn hadn't broken yet. It was March, and spring would be coming soon. The winter would come to an end, and with it, the snow and cold weather would cease. It was time for the sunlight, and warmth, and green, growing things again. This winter had lasted too long.

26

TENNESSEE EVIDENCE

"I should have waited until daylight to call you," Troy said apologetically. "I knew there wasn't anything we'd be able to do until daylight."

Susan Callahan shook her head. "No," she answered. "You called when you had information and we were ready for daylight. We've made the contacts. Now we wait. Once we get some information back, we'll go to the court and get the search—"

The phone rang. Susan answered. She sounded as she always did, impassive, unemotional. Troy wondered how she maintained such a manner. He felt the adrenaline coursing through him and even though he'd already been awake for seven hours, he wasn't tired. Tonight, it would probably hit him and he wouldn't be able to stay awake over supper. But now, he was on alert and ready. Finally, thanks to Kelly, they had a real lead.

Susan's answers to the telephone message were spoken in a brief monotone. When she hung up the phone, Troy, who was seated on the edge of her desk, waited.

"Jessie Sloan's mother died five years ago. Jessie Kay James Sloan hasn't been back home to Jackson's Creek—it's a little country town about fifty miles south of Knoxville—in over five years. The police did some investigating. They were very helpful and very apologetic that they couldn't help us."

"But they have helped us," Troy said. "They prove that Greg Sloan lied when he said he was taking his wife home to her mother."

Susan nodded. Her brown eyes focused on the cell phone that Mr. Porter had found in the library parking lot. There were no phone calls to Jessie Sloan from Wyatt Michaels because Jessie Sloan didn't have a cell phone; Greg Sloan had one, but it was used for business calls.

"There's still no proof," she said.

"No proof that Jessie Sloan and Wyatt Michaels knew each other?"

"Right. We're going without much evidence."

"No one has seen Jessie Sloan in weeks. Maybe months. Kelly saw her in December."

"Others might have seen her."

Troy knew that Susan was playing devil's advocate and she was right to do so. But he was impatient. "Other businesses in Settler Springs use the Sloans to clean for them. The Rancottis use them. Call her."

Susan Callahan raised perfectly arched eyebrows. "I wonder if she'll answer," she murmured as she began punching in the numbers of the Rancotti telephone number. "Mrs. Rancotti, I'm sorry to bother you this early—no, this is about your cleaning company. You use the Sloans? Yes, I know the library also uses them. When is the last time you saw Mrs. Sloan? Mrs. Rancotti, I'm going to put you on speaker so that Officer Kennedy can hear."

Caroline Rancotti's voice, sounding confounded but not hostile, was speaking. "We hired them last year. We hired them when we first moved to Settler Springs; there was still a lot to do and we didn't have time to take care of everything. I didn't always see them, they often cleaned when we weren't there, although that wasn't always possible since our hours in the beginning weren't regular. I think it annoyed Greg. Nothing annoys Jessie, she's so easygoing."

"Mrs. Rancotti, when did you see Mrs. Sloan last?"

"I don't know . . . in February, Greg Sloan came in to tell me that his wife was pregnant. They'd been trying for a long time after all her miscarriages—"

"Mrs. Sloan, it's important. Can you remember when you last saw Jessie Sloan?"

A pause. "I suppose it's been awhile. Like I said, we didn't expect to see them."

"Mrs. Sloan, can you possibly narrow down the date when you last saw Mrs. Sloan? The month if not the date?"

"Why? Has something happened to Jessie?"

"When did you last see her?"

"Let me ask Keith. He's better at remembering dates than I am."

They waited, Susan with no expression on her face, Troy feeling tethered to the desk when he wanted to be moving into action.

"This is Keith. You wanted to know when we last saw Jessie Sloan?" he asked, bewilderment in his voice. "Caroline told you that we didn't always see them. They have a key, they can come in when it's convenient. Actually, they won't be coming in. Greg left a phone message last week to say that he's staying in Tennessee with his wife during her pregnancy and he's going to relocate his business."

"Did he say anything else about his move?"

"Only that he had closed up the house."

"I see."

"I suppose he gave all his clients the same message. Why? Has something happened?"

"Do you remember when you last saw Mrs. Sloan?"

"It was awhile ago . . . before Christmas. It was the fall. Before Thanksgiving. Earlier. I'm sorry, it's hard to remember. It was a hectic time."

"Mr. Rancotti, I realize that these are not easy questions, but honest answers may help us to find out who killed Wyatt Michaels. I assume you will be honest with your answers?"

"I've been honest all along," he said.

"You were not honest when you denied knowing the identity of the man in the photograph. Now, you last saw Jessie Sloan before Thanksgiving. When you saw her, was your wife still romantically involved with Mr. Michaels?"

Keith Rancotti didn't answer right away. Troy wondered if Caroline was next to him while he was on the phone and realized that she probably was.

"Yes," he said. "They—I didn't know yet, I hadn't figured it out. It ended soon after that."

"Thank you. Is there any way that Jessie Sloan could have met Wyatt Michaels around that time?"

"I—why?"

They heard Caroline's voice but couldn't distinguish her words.

"Mr. Rancotti, we're trying to solve this case and we need your help. Could Jessie Sloan and Wyatt Michaels have been at your Settler Springs winery at the same time?"

"I suppose so," he said. "We were so busy, unpacking, getting things in order. Michaels was around a lot, doing his story, he said. The Sloans were helping with the cleaning, it was a little more than what they normally do, but they understood that we wanted to be operating before the Christmas holidays. We paid them extra, of course."

"Did you ever notice, was there any time, when Mrs. Sloan and Mr. Michaels were engaged in a conversation? What?"

They heard Caroline's voice.

"Caroline said they were talking about beer. The Sloans brew their own, and she was joking with Michaels about switching his writing from wine to beer. Wait, Caroline wants to say something."

"Just put it on speaker," Susan said. "Then we'll all hear."

"Jessie was always friendly with everyone," Caroline said. Her voice revealed embarrassment. "Greg was downstairs and she was upstairs with us. Usually, almost always, they were together. But he wasn't there and she and Wyatt started talking. I—I noticed."

"I see," Susan said in her imperturbable manner. Caroline had noticed and had likely been jealous. Was it that reaction that had triggered awareness in her husband, or had he already sensed that something was going on in their marriage? *How would he react,* Troy wondered, *if he thought Kelly was unfaithful to him.*

Not well. But Kelly . . . he knew her well enough to sense that if she was feeling restless in their marriage, she'd go to Rev. Dal for guidance before she'd surrender to temptation. For Kelly, faith was a bedrock. He was grateful for that.

"Did you suspect that anything was going on between them?"

"No! I mean, she and Greg . . . I didn't think that."

"But shortly after that, you broke it off with Mr. Michaels. How did he handle it?"

"He was perfectly composed. I don't think it was any more than a fling to him. Was he carrying on with Jessie Sloan?"

"Mrs. Rancotti, this is a murder investigation and I remind you that you are still under suspicion. We're following through on other leads. In the meantime, I expect you and Mr. Rancotti to treat all these questions with confidentiality. I don't want to read about this in the papers and I don't want to learn that rumors have started."

"No, no, I won't—I won't. I just—Jessie Sloan, she's a nice woman. I like her. I hope she didn't fall for Wyatt's line like I did."

"Thank you, Mrs. Rancotti."

"You'll—can you let us know if you, if there's anything that you find out?"

"We're still investigating."

Susan Callahan wouldn't promise any more than that, but after she ended the call, she said, "It sounds like the Rancottis are going to come through this."

"Maybe."

"What's your take?"

Troy shrugged and drank a sip of the coffee he'd bought from a convenience store two hours ago. It was cold.

"Michaels played around. He had a fling with Caroline, found Jessie Sloan interesting, didn't cause a scene when Caroline broke it off because he was already pursuing Jessie. Maybe they met at the library, maybe they left messages for each other. Maybe Jessie was infatuated with him. Country girl, all of a sudden meets someone from the city. When he came to the wine and cheese gig, it wasn't to see Caroline. He left after an hour and he didn't interview anyone about the wines they were sampling. Maybe he'd gotten the information he needed."

"That's plausible. It's speculative, but it's plausible. We can't interview Wyatt Michaels, he's dead. We can't interview Jessie Sloan because we don't know where she is. We haven't been able to talk to Greg Sloan because no one answers at his number and his mailbox is full."

"I think that's enough for the judge."

"I think so too. Let's go."

27

HOW IT HAPPENED

"**H**e said he loved her."

Troy didn't know which was more troubling: the discovery of human remains buried on Greg Sloan's property, the bloodstains in the garage that weren't quite gone despite the bleach that had been poured on the concrete floor, or the calm demeanor of the man who had been extradited by Tennessee law enforcement and was now in custody.

Susan Callahan was letting Greg Sloan do the talking. Silence didn't bother her. It didn't bother Greg Sloan either. He was willing to talk.

"She was my wife. She wasn't his to love. She was mine. I loved her."

"When did you discover that Mrs. Sloan was being unfaithful to you?"

Greg Sloan didn't look at either of the officers. He looked straight ahead, not dodging their queries. "She told me in December that she thought she was pregnant. I was happy. She was too. She had trouble carrying a child past the first three months. I didn't want her to take any chances. I said I'd do the cleaning. I didn't want her to be around chemicals. We were always together. We shared the business. It's in both our names. That was only fair. We both shared the work. But I wanted us to be careful, for the baby. So I said I'd do the cleaning. We do a lot of cleaning in the evening, into the night. A couple of times, I came home and she wasn't there. We only have the one truck. She would come home, someone dropped her off. At first, I didn't think much of it. I didn't know of any friends she had, but . . . she said she was at church meetings and I figured someone from church dropped her off. I thought it was a good thing, her getting more active in the church now that she had the free time to do so. It would be good for the baby. Then . . . I don't know. Something was different. I'd be cleaning the library, and I'd start to notice things. I do a thorough job when I clean," he told them earnestly. "I earn my paycheck. I started finding things like notes."

"What did the notes say?"

"Sometimes not more than a time and a place. 9:15, Tuesday, library. I thought it was kids at first, but then I started to wonder. The notes were in the Children's Room. Sometimes that room needs extra cleaning. The kids leave things, they pull out the books, they play with the toys. The children's librarian isn't full time, she doesn't always have the chance to tidy up. I started noticing that the notes were left around that shelf with the characters on it."

"Raggedy Ann?" Troy asked.

Greg nodded. "It started to get more frequent, and I started to wonder. So one night, instead of going to my cleaning job, I drove to the library and sat outside. Tuesday night is my late night, that's when I clean the industrial complex in Kensington City and I'm gone longer. Most of the night; I don't get home until after 11, sometimes midnight. I waited outside. I saw them go into the library."

"When was this?"

"January."

"Mr. Sloan, it's dark in January by that time of night. How could you be sure that it was your wife and Mr.

Michaels going into the library?" Susan asked patiently.

"I know what my wife looks like in the dark."

"And Mr. Michaels? How could you be sure it was him?"

"I'd seen him at the winery. The Rancottis are our clients."

"What time did they leave the library?"

"Ten-thirty."

"They weren't there very long," Troy remarked.

"They weren't checking out books. They didn't turn the lights on," Greg Sloan answered.

"What did you do?"

"I drove around, then I went home around the time I'd usually be there on a Tuesday. She was in bed. I asked her where she'd been. She didn't expect that question. She said she'd been home. I told her I knew better. I told her not to lie to me. She said she wanted a divorce. She wanted to leave me for this guy. I said I had to meet him. She arranged a meeting."

"Where did you meet?"

"I met him at his place. He lives in Pittsburgh. An apartment. Nice place. Not the kind of place I could see Jessie liking. She likes the outdoors. This was fancy. Paintings on the wall, expensive TV . . . not Jessie's style. I noticed that he was growing a beard. He didn't look so elegant, not like he'd looked when I first saw him at the winery. Jessie likes men with beards. That's when I knew. And then he told me that he loved her and he wanted to marry her."

"What did you say?"

"I said no. She's my wife. Marriage is forever. We were expecting our baby."

"Was it your child?"

"I thought it was. Then I didn't know. By February, I knew I couldn't stand it anymore. I told Jessie she had to give him up. I'd forgive her, I said, but this had to stop. I was in the pits of hell that winter, never knowing what she might be doing. They stopped meeting at the library but I knew they were still seeing each other. I couldn't stand it. I'd think of the two of them together and I'd feel like my head was filled with hellfire. She came home one night, I hadn't gone to clean, I just couldn't. She didn't expect to see me. I knew she'd been with him."

"What did you do?"

"I killed her."

"How?"

"I put my arms around her throat and I just kept squeezing until she stopped fighting me. Then I knew that she wasn't going to see him any more. I buried her body by the tree in the back, that's where we used to have picnics. I figured it would be peaceful for her."

"How did Mr. Michaels find out?"

"I called him and told him to come out. I said I wanted to talk to him, man to man. Jessie was out, I told him that he and I needed to talk. He came. He must have thought that I would give her up. I poured us both beers. Jessie and I brew our own beer. I knew what I needed to do. I had gotten sleeping pills from the doctor. I just couldn't sleep. I emptied a couple of the capsules into his drink. He said it tasted bad. I said it was home-brewed beer and he just wasn't used to a real man's beer. So he drank it all just to prove that he was a man. He got kind of groggy. He's a big guy, strong, too. I stabbed him and dragged his body out to the garage. I cleaned up my place the best I could; then I cleaned the garage. It was the day of the snowstorm."

"Did you plan to kill them when you heard the weather forecast?"

"I didn't plan to kill Jessie. I just couldn't go on like we were and she wouldn't leave him. The snow hadn't gotten here yet. It was Wednesday night. When I heard the forecast, I knew that was the time to do it. I was worried that he wouldn't show because of the weather, but he came out in the daytime on Thursday, before the snow hit."

"Why did you bring his body to the library?"

"Where else was I going to put him? I wasn't going to go to the trouble of burying him and I didn't want him in the ground near Jessie. The snow hadn't started yet, but it was like everything had stopped. People hunkered down like they do. Even the library closed early. No one was out and the snow hadn't started to fall yet. But no one was around. I knew no one would know that I'd been in the library. I knew how things were arranged in the library, you see."

"You chose that section of the library to leave his body?"

"I looked up adultery in the catalog," he said. "I wanted him to be put where he belonged. There was a book titled *The Seventh Commandment.* I put his body there."

"What about your wife's wedding ring?"

"You found that? I didn't think anyone would. I put it there, by that book. That's where it belonged because she'd broken the seventh commandment, 'Thou shalt not commit adultery'."

"And her engagement ring?"

"I put that upstairs in the Children's Corner. It fit perfectly around that little ceramic figure of Tinker Bell, you know, she's the little fairy in *Peter Pan*."

"You didn't choose that character intentionally?"

Greg Sloan shook his head. "Her engagement ring, the ring I got her, it fit right around the little statue. I left it there."

"Did you ever check out books from the library?"

"I took out some books on cheaters. I thought maybe there would be an answer there, something I could tell her to make her stop. But there wasn't anything in them. I left them in the book drop so no one would know I had taken them. I didn't steal them. I brought them back."

"Did you leave wine glasses there?"

"Wine glasses? Oh, yeah, I did. I'd forgotten about those." He rubbed his eyes. "I was mad then. That was a while ago."

"Mr. Sloan, you know why you're here?"

"I know. I killed my wife. I killed her lover. I didn't think I'd be found. I left Settler Springs on Thursday. I got lucky; the ladies closed the library early, even before it started snowing. After I killed him, I put his jacket back on and I put him in my truck. I wrapped him in a tarp. If someone saw me, they wouldn't think anything of it; everyone knows I clean for the library. But no one saw me. I went in the back door. No one was in the parking lot. I carried his body over my shoulders. I put him down in the section where that book about adultery was. I put the rings where I told you. And I left."

"What if someone had seen you?"

"They didn't."

"What if one of the library staff came back for something?"

"They didn't. No one saw me. Except you, Officer Kennedy."

"Me? I wasn't in town. I was at a conference, miles away."

Greg Sloan nodded his head. "I was the guy with the flat tire, off the exit ramp. You stopped to see if I needed help. I recognized you, but you didn't recognize me. You offered me brownies that your wife made for you." He shook his head as if he was scolding Troy. "You shouldn't have done that. She made them for you. Not for another man."

28

LOVE REMAINS

It was a sober service but in its own way, a purifying one. Rev. Dal Meacham was not the pastor of the church where Jessie was a member, but he had agreed immediately when Kelly asked him perform the funeral over Jessie's exhumed body. Her own minister was too shaken by the news that Greg Sloan had killed his wife and he gratefully accepted Rev. Dal's offer to do the service in his stead.

The Rancottis were there, standing close to each other as if they were sheltering one another from the buffeting fortunes of marriage gone awry. Troy was there in a suit and tie, next to Kelly in a dark dress. Trooper Susan Callahan was in uniform, a reminder of the manner in which Jessie had been killed. Chloe and Carmela came together; Mr. Porter stood with them, his dignified face somber as he listened to the words of the service.

Rev. Dal read from First Corinthians, boldly choosing the Love Chapter of the Bible to bury a woman for whom love had gone horribly wrong. "Love is patient; love is kind; love is not envious or boastful or arrogant or rude. It does not insist on its own way; it is not irritable or resentful; it does not rejoice in wrongdoing, but rejoices in the truth. It bears all things, believes all things, hopes all things, endures all things. Love never ends. But as for prophecies, they will come to an end; as for tongues, they will cease; as for knowledge, it will come to an end. For we know only in part, and we prophesy only in part; but when the complete comes, the partial will come to an end."

He closed his Bible and continued reciting from memory. "Now I know only in part; then I will know fully, even as I have been fully known. And now faith, hope, and love abide, these three; and the greatest of these is love.' Our community has been shaken by the death of Jessie Sloan, a woman known to many of us as someone who was kind and gentle. She is with God now, where violence and harm can no longer reach her. Let us remember her as she was in life and as we treasure the ones we love, let us remember what Paul tells us about love. Notice that he tells us what love is not. Many couples choose this scripture for their weddings, but they fail to live it. There is no magic formula for love. All of us, at some time in our relationships and our marriages, have found the burdens of our vows more than we feel we can bear. We doubt that we are loved in the way that we want to be loved, or we cannot give the love that our spouse or partner seeks. These are human limitations. God's love is stronger, more powerful, more enduring, than anything that we can extend to one another. Paul sees the context of our perceptions. 'when the complete comes, the partial will come to an end.' Brothers and sisters in Christ, we live in the partial. The best of us, the most loving, the most attentive, we still live and love in the partial. Only God's love is whole. Born as we are into the sin of Adam and Eve, we must struggle so that we do not imprison one another in our partial love. Surrender to God first, and accept the love that He gives you. Jessie Sloan is beloved of God in whole. Take that for comfort."

There was no luncheon after the service; this was not a traditional funeral. It was more of a catharsis, Troy thought as he took Kelly's arm to leave the gravesite.

They hadn't gotten very far before someone called Kelly's name. She turned to see Caroline Rancotti coming toward her.

"Kelly, I'm sorry," Caroline said hurriedly. "I said some awful things. I just—"

"We're sorry," Keith said.

Kelly nodded. "I hope you'll reconsider leaving Settler Springs," she said. "There's a place for your family here, I'm sure of it."

"I—we're thinking. About a lot of things." Caroline looked to Troy. "What will happen to her husband?"

"He'll go to prison. The psychiatrists have evaluated him. He knows what he did was wrong, but he feels it was justified because they were married and she was unfaithful." Troy knew that these would be blunt words for the Rancottis, but Rev. Dal's words were still fresh. *Loving in partial.* Greg Sloan loved his wife, but his love wasn't whole. When she found someone else, he retaliated so that she couldn't give herself to another man. He thought that brownies made by a wife couldn't be given to another man; an outrageous stance surely, but it was the only thing that explained his actions when he found out that Jessie had taken a lover. And had fallen in love with him. And, apparently, Wyatt Michaels had fallen in love with Jessie. Partial love, because she was married and he was a philanderer. "I don't understand it," Troy said candidly. "That's why I'm a cop and not a psychiatrist."

The Rancottis nodded in unison. "I guess we'd better stick to wine," Caroline said with a hesitant laugh. "It's what we know."

When they were in the car, Kelly said, "I still don't get it. Why did Jessie want to read that article that he'd written? It had nothing to do with her."

"Susan thinks she was infatuated with Wyatt. Like teenage girls when they get infatuated with a boy. She said they want to know everything about him, and they want to talk about him, say his name . . . she thinks that's why Jessie wanted to read the article."

"Maybe I should read it. Maybe it would bring clarity to this."

"Susan read it. She said it's just about wine. There's nothing in it that gives any hints about what he was really thinking or feeling. Maybe he did fall in love with Jessie Sloan and maybe they would have gotten married."

"There are a lot of things that still don't make sense to me. What if we hadn't closed the library early?

The snow hadn't started yet; I rushed things. I just didn't want to be there, listening to people talk about how bad the storm was going to be when I thought at the time that you'd be driving home in it. So we closed. And he killed Wyatt Michaels in the daytime, came here, no one saw him. He left the body in the romance fiction section where *The Seventh Commandment* was shelved. What if we hadn't been closed?"

"He'd have waited. He wanted to leave Michaels' body there. He had no real reason to go to Tennessee, except that's where Jessie came from and I think maybe he was on some kind of a pilgrimage. I don't know how he recognized me when I stopped to help him with the flat tire. I didn't see him clearly."

"But he knew who you are. You didn't know him. You wouldn't have recognized him."

"Nobody recognized him, in the end," Troy remarked. "He wasn't what they thought."

"It makes me unsettled. I just want spring to come," Kelly sighed. "This winter has been horrible. I want it to be spring."

"It's just about here."

"Yes, but spring takes so long to make its mark," she said.

Troy turned the Suburban onto the street by the library.

"Oh, look! It's Lucas!"

"Who's the girl?"

"That's Maddie. They're almost the same height," she said happily.

"What?"

"Oh, before Valentine's Day, Lucas was bothered because he was shorter than she is. And now, he's taller."

"Okayyyy . . . I guess this all makes sense to you?" Troy inquired, laughing because it was a riddle to him.

"Yes," Kelly said. "Spring is definitely coming."

THANK YOU FOR CHOOSING A PUREREAD BOOK!

We hope you enjoyed the story, and as a way to thank you for choosing PureRead we'd like to send you this free Special Edition Cozy, and other fun reader rewards...

Click Here to download your free Cozy Mystery
PureRead.com/cozy

Thanks again for reading.

See you soon!

OTHER BOOKS IN THIS SERIES

If you loved this story why not continue straight away
with other books in the series?

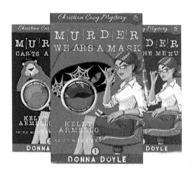

Murder Wears A Mask

Murder Casts a Shadow

Murder Plans The Menu

Murder Wears a Medal

Murder Is A Smoking Gun

Murder Has a Heart

OR READ THE COMPLETE BOXSET!

Start Reading On Amazon Now

OUR GIFT TO YOU

AS A WAY TO SAY THANK YOU WE WOULD
LOVE TO SEND YOU THIS SPECIAL EDITION
COZY MYSTERY FREE OF CHARGE.

Our Reader List is 100% FREE

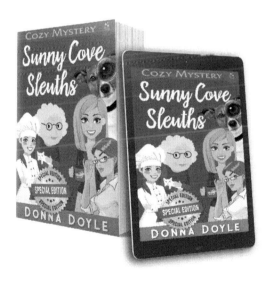

Click Here to download your free Cozy Mystery
PureRead.com/cozy

At PureRead we publish books you can trust. Great tales without smut or swearing, but with all of the mystery and romance you expect from a great story.

Be the first to know when we release new books, take part in our fun competitions, and get surprise free books in your inbox by signing up to our Reader list.

As a thank you you'll receive this exclusive Special Edition Cozy available only to our subscribers...

Click Here to download your free Cozy Mystery
PureRead.com/cozy

Thanks again for reading.
See you soon!

Made in the USA
Coppell, TX
15 November 2023

24291657R00164